MW00892670

LEGENDS OF THE DONUT SHOP

Terry Overton

The Stories They Left for Us to Tell

© **2022 Terry Overton**

Other books by Terry Overton:
Both Sides of the Border, Ambassador International
Oddball Ornaments: Story of Christmas, Ambassador International
America of We the People, Independently Published
Devotional for Youth, CPH
Devotional for Caregivers, CPH
Devotional for Those Coping with Tragedy, CPH

Coming Soon:

Sabal Palms and the Southern Squall, Ambassador International
Sabal Palms After the Storm, Ambassador International
Sabal Palms Tales of the Fall Equinox, Ambassador International
Oddball Ornaments: Story of Forgiveness, Ambassador International
The Newton Chronicles Series, Ambassador International

In Loving Memory of My Parents

Kenneth F. Meier, September 23, 1932---March 10, 2022

&

Jerry Meier, August 31, 1932—March 9, 2022

Semper Fi

Preface

The story I am going to tell you happened when I was a teenager. At the age of seventeen, following a tragic accident, I had an experience that changed my life. This experience included a very special place in my hometown. This place didn't look like anything special on the outside. It was what happened on the inside that mattered.

Like thousands of other towns, our town has a Donut Shop not far from Main Street. In small coffee shops, donut shops, and cafés, all over the country, groups of men or women meet weekly just to enjoy each other's company and talk about current events or of days gone by while they enjoy breakfast. The Donut Shop in the town where I lived was just one of those places, and my grandfather belonged to one of those groups of men. These men had lived their lives in hard times of poverty and war and became all the better for it. They were the men who made this great country. They were the heroes of wars and solid citizens who contributed to our world.

On weekends and holidays, I was lucky enough to tag along with my grandfather for breakfast with his buddies at the Donut Shop. I wish I had appreciated it more when I went with him to eat the donuts, sip coffee, and hear the tales told by older men who accepted me as one of their own family members.

CHAPTER ONE

Near Death

This wasn't how it was supposed to be. There was no dark tunnel with a light at the end, like people say. There were no angels in long white gowns singing, no trumpets sounding, no harps playing. Billowing silver clouds had not opened to pull me into a heavenly eternity. No Saint Peter stood waiting for me at the pearly gates. It was just me floating above the bed for what seemed like an eternity.

I hovered over my own hospital bed in the dark, sterile room and looked down on my unresponsive body, arms poking out from crisp white sheets. Overwhelmed with fear, I was powerless to do anything. I couldn't move my limbs or talk. Hooked up to tubes pumping fluids into my arms and wires connected to my chest, my body was lifeless. How did I get here?

Abruptly, everything had changed. I didn't know how. Yet here I was, Wes Williams, in a hospital bed lying as still as a rock. The beeping sounds of metal machines and abundant wires connected to noisy digital displays filled the room. My parents anxiously looked over my bed and whispered in sad tones to the doctor. My current reality terrified me.

Moments of utter darkness and hazy fog passed. Then, the obscure blackness was at once replaced with a warm, shimmering glow of some sort. Inside and out, I had an undeniable sense that I was at last heaven bound. But I didn't go anywhere. I remained in the hospital room.

I looked down at my lifeless body and waited to be lifted into the heavens. My mother and father gasped, and tears rolled down their cheeks.

I glanced between my worried parents and my limp, unconscious body and wondered about the other folk tales I'd heard. Where was the "life flashing before my eyes" part? Nope, I was stuck up here, looking down. I was weightless, as light as the bloom of a milkweed plant floating in the breeze of a summer day.

The doctor's raspy older voice provided an update. "There is some internal bleeding in the abdominal area. He's losing quite a bit of blood. We'll need to take him down to the operating room again as soon as the table is ready."

Hold on! The doctor said I am going to the operating room *again*? I've *already* had an operation? What for?

My dad mumbled, "Is he going to be okay?"

The doctor looked at my dad, then placed his hand on my mom's shoulder. "My team will do everything we can."

I heard more sobbing from my parents. Dad held Mom who cried uncontrollably with her head buried in his shoulder. Now, Dad cried.

I regretted seeing them so upset. I wanted to reach down and touch Mom on the shoulder and say, "Wait, I'm right here. I'm still here. I'm not going anywhere. Don't worry, Mom. It's going to be okay. I'm still here, Dad." I attempted to reach Mom, but I was too far above her. In my mind, I moved my arm toward her, but nothing happened.

My mom stood at my bedside, took my hand, and squeezed. "Wes, Weston, don't go…"

I thought she wanted to say something more, but she was crying. Her voice, between a whisper and a mumble, made it impossible for me to understand her words.

I felt another strange sensation. My past life was before me, but not like I expected it. There was no vision of my life passing by like a speeding train. There were no flashbacks of things I thought important, like little league baseball trophies, track meet ribbons, honor roll report cards, or that perfect school attendance certificate from the fourth grade that hung on my bedroom wall next to my bookcase. There was nothing about beginning my senior year of high school, my first part-time job, or even my friends.

Somehow, I was elsewhere. I'd been transported to another location. I wasn't in the present. I was back in my earlier years and in the one place that felt more like home than my own house. No longer suspended in the hospital room, I wondered, *Why here? Why am I in this particular place?*

I smiled at the thought of this place. Seeing it was weird. It was strange because I saw a younger version of myself. I must have been eleven or twelve years old, maybe thirteen at the most. Through the glass window of the door, there I was. My younger self took hold of the handle on the outside, opened it, and stepped inside. This small café was where I had achieved nothing at all on my own. This place was different. This was where my heart was filled with warmth and admiration for all the people in the room.

Time shifted again to present day. Back in the hospital, my body was jostled about. I was moved from one hospital bed to a flatter bed. A nurse pulled up the metal rails on the bed. Three nurses rolled me out of the room and down the hallway.

Was I dead? Was it over?

I floated above my body as they wheeled me down the dimly lit, long, stark hallway. One of the overhead lights made a strange buzzing noise as I floated past. The wheels of this flatter bed screeched and bumped on cracks in the tile floor. The hospital staff rolled me along and hustled as if their lives depended on getting somewhere at the speed of light. I suppose this was a good thing because it meant I wasn't yet gone from the earth. If I had already died, they wouldn't be in such a hurry.

I witnessed as they pulled my bed into another room and lifted my body on to a metal table. It was a different type of room. The room smelled of rubbing alcohol, medicines, and cleaning fluids.

Was I still breathing? I couldn't tell. My first thought was: *this must be the morgue.*

"Be careful," one nurse said to another.

The words of caution indicated my life was not over. I couldn't feel the needle, but I watched it enter just at my shoulder.

The nurses hooked up multiple machines, and the beeping began again. Intense lights pointed directly at my body. Two nurses draped the crinkly paper sheets crisscross over me. Only a small portion of my body, maybe my stomach or abdomen, was exposed as far as I could tell. My view from above the bed was blocked by the lights, making it difficult to watch what was happening below. The doctor maneuvered sharp metal instruments, causing an unusual clinking noise each time he put one down and took another.

I felt another airy sensation as I floated around the operating room. It felt almost peaceful. I dozed off. Darkness. Quiet at last.

Had I been asleep an hour? Ten minutes? Was I dead? No way I could know.

Time shifted. I was again back in my childhood at the same place. I opened the door and entered the small but warm room with a wooden floor that creaked with every step of a cowboy boot but remained silent for my sneakers. The bright sunlight streamed through the window as it always did in the early morning. I wanted to stay here. I didn't want to go back to the operating room to wonder if I would live or die. I was here and wanted to stay awhile at this place—*The Donut Shop*, my favorite place in the whole world.

CHAPTER TWO

My Favorite Place

It must have been either a Saturday, a holiday, or summertime because, otherwise, I would have been in school. There I was, the middle-school version of me. I walked into this place where the air smelled like sugar. The wonderful warm donuts with a variety of gooey toppings were not the reason I loved to come here. It was all the adventures and places I visited in my mind when I listened to the stories.

There he was, walking into the shop right behind me. My grandfather. The other regulars—Jimmy, Parker, Old Walt, and Lawson—were already sitting around the table. I knew, whether I lived through this surgery or died, I didn't care. Somehow, I had been given one final visit to my favorite place on earth with the people who, as it turned out, would be the most important people of my life. At my middle school age, I hadn't yet understood how important this place was. But later, I would find out.

I watched the younger me as I took my usual seat at the table with five other men. They considered me one of the men at these gatherings. They told me stories like I was a grown-up. Even though this earlier version of me was years away from shaving my face, these men accepted me as one of their own.

I looked at my grandfather. He was healthy and walking upright. He didn't know a few years later he would undergo hip replacement surgery which would have severe complications and leave him unable to walk on his own. In this space and time, my grandfather could get around just fine. He towered over me and, since he didn't need a walker like he would after his surgery, he looked as strong as the day he went to Marine Boot Camp at Fort Pendleton. At least, that was how I perceived him. Broad shoulders, salt and pepper hair, muscular arms, and the Marine Corps tattoo on his forearm. Yep. I remembered when he looked just like this. He was my role model and, besides my own father, the strongest male figure in my life.

My grandfather waved to the owner as he sat down. "Good morning, Jae."

Jae smiled, waved back, and nodded. Her nod indicated she was getting my grandfather a bear claw and, for me, two glazed donuts and one donut with chocolate icing. Jae scurried to our table and brought our plates of warm sugary donuts and two empty coffee mugs, which she filled right away with the hot, steamy beverage. As a middle schooler, having a cup of coffee with these men around the table was a sign of complete acceptance.

Jae had an interesting name. She was from Korea, and my grandfather told me her name meant talented or respected or something like that. I didn't understand Korean names and their meanings. The relationship Jae had with my grandfather and his friends was unusual. Why? Three of the men, including my grandfather, were in the Korean War. But that's another whole story.

Jimmy sat across from us. Gesturing toward my grandfather, Jimmy asked, "Jae, why did you let that old scallywag in?"

Calling my grandfather a scallywag was nothing new for Jimmy. Marine Corps grunts, like Granddad, and regular Army joes, like Jimmy, had an ongoing rivalry. It was all in good fun. They respected each other and defended each other in any situation. But here at the Donut Shop, as they ate their delicious breakfast, they often bantered and called each other names.

My grandfather scratched his beard. "Well, Jimmy, to tell you truth, I didn't know you'd be here, or I wouldn't have come."

Jimmy looked exactly as I remembered. He reminded me of an old salty sea captain. I have no clue why. Maybe it was his thick white beard and rough, well-sunned face. Here he was at the Donut Shop and looking as healthy as ever. Jimmy didn't know he would die shortly after I turned seventeen. Granddad would later tell me it was cancer that killed him. Jimmy wouldn't find out he had the disease until it was too late. And he fought it to the very end, making his way to the Donut Shop up to the last week before he died. We all cried. It was amazing to see Jimmy again, joking and laughing with Granddad.

Wherever I was in this strange dimension of time, Jimmy was still alive, and my grandfather walked upright. It brought great happiness to my heart.

The men around the table laughed and sipped their coffee between bites of donuts.

Old Walter, who sat next to me, winked, patted my arm, and said, "Young man, you look like you could use a few more donuts." He laughed and pushed a plate full of donut holes my way.

These grandfather-aged men relentlessly beckoned me to gain weight. Old Walter never missed a chance to try to fatten me up. I wondered if I looked thin or if it was because his body was the shape of a pear and at least forty pounds overweight. Never one to pass on a donut hole, I put one on my plate.

Old Walter's leathery face crumpled as he laughed harder when I grabbed the donut hole. Old Walt was a rancher. Working cattle in the elements year after year had taken a toll on his face. The crevices and deep creases were the most noticeable when he smiled. His face squashed up so much it looked like a withered-up horse apple.

My grandfather came up with the nickname "Old Walter" years ago to protest Old Walter's attempt to call his son Walter Junior. My grandfather said, "Now don't stick that boy with a junior at the end of his name! He'd be dragging that junior attachment around all his life. Like an extra-heavy suitcase! We all know he's just a youngster, and you are just old, Walter. Plain and simple. And that's what we will call you from now on. Old Walter. In fact, we'll shorten your name and call you Old Walt."

Old Walt tried for months to call his son Walter Junior, but Granddad would have none of that. Whenever Old Walt mentioned Walter Junior, my hardheaded grandfather would ask,

"Who is this junior you keep bringing up, Old Walt? You're not talking about that little boy who follows you around?"

I'm not sure Old Walter accepted his new name of "Old Walt," but at the Donut Shop, he was called Old Walter or Old Walt, and his son was never called Walter Junior. And that was that. Personally, I believe the reason Old Walt allowed this to happen was because my grandfather and Old Walt were both in the Marines and my grandfather outranked him during their service together. Granddad was a sergeant, and Old Walt was a corporal. Now, both men would say rank didn't matter to them anymore, but out of respect, I think it mattered to Old Walt. One thing was for certain —if any of these five men needed anything under the sun, he could count on the others in the Donut Shop group for help. It was the unspoken code.

Old Walt worked with all kinds of people on his large cattle ranch not far from town. He had plenty of stories about them all. From time to time, he had hired drifters, rambling ranch hands, bronco riders who were injured in the rodeo, and at least one runaway horse thief. Old Walt's worth was estimated to be in the millions of dollars. But his beat-up boots and worn cowboy hat never gave an inkling of a hint of his bank account. His shirts were clean and pressed, and his jeans never had a tear or hole. One time, Granddad tried to take up donations to buy Old Walt a new cowboy hat. Walt refused and said his hat was more valuable because it was an antique. I figured he was telling the truth.

Jimmy, when he was living, had a small farm not far from Old Walt's place. He kept the yard immaculate, and he was outside in a flash if a leaf dared to fall into the flower bed or a weed attempted to emerge. He proudly flew Old Glory on a rod attached to a wooden column on his front porch. Every day, he watched the weather forecast so he'd know when the weather was changing in case he needed to put the flag away to keep it dry when it rained or snowed.

Parker, also a Marine, lived next to Jimmy. He and Jimmy were probably about the same age, but Parker looked younger. Sometimes the group called him Baby-faced Parker, which Parker did not like. But Parker was the most reserved of the bunch, and when they referred to him as having a baby face, he just shrugged his shoulders and changed the topic of conversation. I thought the gang could call Parker just about any name and he would react the same way with a simple shrug of the shoulders. For a Marine, he was about the most soft-spoken one I'd ever met.

My grandfather lived in a small brick house just inside the town limits. I stayed there on the weekends when Mom and Dad worked. Since the men were scattered all about the county, the Donut Shop was the perfect meeting spot. It was my favorite place in town. There was never a calm moment when the group of men, Old Walt, Parker, Lawson, Jimmy, and my grandfather, got together for breakfast. When they gathered in the mornings, and I had the chance to listen to their tales of an earlier era, the rest of the day felt full of promise and future adventures.

CHAPTER THREE

Lawson

I remained in this alternate time, watching myself as a middle school kid. On another beautiful sunny Saturday morning, Granddad and I drove to breakfast.

"'Bout time you two showed up," Jimmy hollered.

"We had to get ready. Can't rush beauty, you know," Granddad replied. "And from the looks of it, it looks like you got dressed in less than five minutes. Did you even comb your hair?"

"I don't need to get all spruced up. My good looks are all-natural."

Jimmy and Granddad both laughed.

Old Walt, Parker, and Lawson, already in the middle of their donut eating routine, kept eating as if no conversation was happening between my grandfather and Jimmy. Granddad and I picked up our prepared plates of donuts and cups of coffee from the counter and took a seat. We hadn't been in the Donut Shop long enough to finish our first donut when Jae brought refills of coffee. The rest of the group remained quiet once we sat down. I looked around the table at Granddad's buddies. By the time I had reached middle school, I knew each of them pretty well.

My grandfather, Old Walt, Parker, and Jimmy were friends years before Lawson moved to town. Jimmy and Old Walt lived near each other. Just down the road from Jimmy's place was Lawson's house, a small farmhouse with a big porch. Lawson said he liked the property because it had a few pine trees on the back of the land, which was not typical in that part of Texas. He said the small hills, rolling landscape, and pine trees reminded him of his home in Virginia.

"Thinking I'll plant a dogwood tree this year," Lawson announced.

"Why? Why plant it here? It might not do well." Old Walt was stumped.

"It's the state tree," Lawson stated.

"Not this state," Old Walt declared.

"No, but it is the state tree of Virginia," Lawson argued. "It will remind me of my home state."

"Well, sir, in this home state, the state tree is the pecan tree. You know, a tree you can use to make pies, cookies, and pralines. What can you do with a dogwood? Eat the flowers?"

Everyone around the table broke out in laughter

Lawson looked quite a bit older than my grandfather. From the looks of him, I thought he might be ten years older. His face wasn't as wrinkled as Old Walt's worn-out ranch face, but his body looked frailer than my grandfather's. He had spent a good deal of his life inside the sheriff's office or a sheriff's vehicle. He had a long history of stories about law enforcement, and he told his stories to anyone who would listen. He frequently talked to people when they were busy doing something else. I had seen him stop the mailman, neighbors, shop owners, and bank clerks, all in the middle of doing their jobs or chores, and thirty minutes later, he was still talking. I thought Lawson seemed either bored or lonely. I figured that was why he talked to everyone.

Every Saturday, and sometimes during the middle of the week, my grandfather met Jimmy, Parker, Old Walt, and Lawson at the Donut Shop. After meeting for so many years, I wondered if they would run out of stories. They never did. Especially Lawson. I never hesitated to ask Lawson a question because I knew he would give me a straight, thorough, and lengthy answer. One of the questions burning in my mind was if he missed his home state so much, why would he ever leave it? I decided it was time to ask him.

"Lawson, why did you move here from Virginia?"

"Wes, after I retired from being sheriff in Virginia, I bought a place next to this scoundrel," he said, nodding toward Jimmy, "to be closer to my grandson. But, like all kids who grow up, my grandson married and moved to Dallas for a job. He and his wife moved to El Paso a few years later. Said he could make more money there."

My grandfather swallowed a bite of his bear claw pastry and said, "Lawson, tell Wes about the time you fought a gorilla."

This was a story I hadn't heard. "A gorilla?"

"Yes, son. A gorilla."

"Why would you do that?"

"After my time in the Navy, I dated this pretty young lady from my hometown. In fact, we would marry a few months later. Anyway, we were out on a date at Porky's Diner downtown and the waitress had just brought out a couple of pulled pork sandwiches. I remember the jukebox was playing 'Bouquet of Roses' by Eddy Arnold. About that time, some men came inside and asked for me by name. The waitress pointed to me. They walked right up and asked me if I could go to Lynchburg that same evening to fight a gorilla."

"Why did they come to find you? Did they know you already?"

"No. But they heard from others that I liked to box. I figured I'd take my date to Lynchburg and impress her. She could watch me fight a gorilla."

This shocked me. "I can't imagine. Those animals are huge and strong. What happened?"

"I beat him."

"Seriously?"

Granddad couldn't stand it. He had to tease Lawson about this. "You only did that to make your girl like you. You had to do something to win her heart."

Lawson laughed. "I can't lie. Seeing her sitting over at the side, smiling so pretty, in that pink sweater, watching me fighting the gorilla in the ring gave me some motivation to win and get out of there."

"Did you win any money?" I asked.

"Nope. Just a blue ribbon. I was a legend back home." He

grinned and winked at me.

"But fighting the gorilla wasn't your only altercation," Granddad teased. "Tell him the rest, you know, about how, as a kid, you never missed an opportunity to fight other kids in your town."

"That's true. I used to get into plenty of skirmishes when I was young. I fought kids all over town. You could say I had a reputation. That was how I came to be a deputy."

"Wait." I held up my hand. "I don't understand. How could someone who was in so many fights become a deputy?"

"The sheriff before I became sheriff asked me if I would assist him by keeping order at a local nightclub. He said he was tired of getting calls at midnight to go kick people out who'd had too much to drink. I said okay. Then he made me a deputy for the weekends at the club. And that was how my law enforcement career started. But all of that happened after I came back from World War Two."

"World War Two? You were in World War Two? No way!"

"I was a gunner's mate and served briefly during the war. In fact, I boxed in the Navy, too. But one fella bigger than me, great big old ugly guy with a beat-up face, cleaned my clock and they put me on a ship the next day."

"Well, we needed a fighter like you out there fighting against the enemy instead of fighting our boys in the ring in the Navy," Old Walt said.

"I didn't fight the enemy too long. The war ended not long after I deployed. "

"Really?" I asked.

"Yes. Once the enemy heard I was in the Navy and on a ship fighting against them, they just up and surrendered."

The men laughed.

Lawson continued exaggerating his tall tale. "Yep. The enemy told President Truman they just didn't have enough ammo or firepower to beat me." Lawson laughed, but the other men shook their heads in disbelief.

Lawson wasn't famous for what he did in the war. And he

wasn't all that famous for the gorilla fight. He was best known for what he did in the 1960s during the Civil Rights protests in his home state of Virginia. But that was a story he told me over breakfast on a different day.

Jae brought a fresh pot of coffee and refilled all the cups once again. The steam quieted when I added a little cold milk to my cup. The others drank their coffee black and mine looked more like a cup of chocolate milk. Each year I added a little less cream and by the time I was a senior in high school, I drank mine black just like the other men.

"More donuts?" Jae asked.

"I might have one more of those cake ones with the cinnamon," Lawson said. "Oh, and I think I need a breakfast sandwich to take home. Makes a good lunch."

"Old Walt, you aren't going over to Fort Worth today, are you?" Granddad asked.

Old Walt swallowed his coffee. "Thought I would."

Jimmy wouldn't let this conversation go on. Just like always, he had to be in the middle of it. "Now, why do you care if Old Walt is going over there?"

"Oh, I don't. He can go wherever he wants. Just wondered if he would be around to help me out with that fence in my backyard," Granddad replied.

"Didn't know your fence needed fixin'," Old Walt said.

"Just told you it did." My grandfather grinned.

Lawson laughed. "You always have something falling apart."

All the men chuckled.

Parker, who had been quiet the entire morning, spoke up. "I reckon that's about right at your age."

The men laughed again.

"I'll help you with the fence, Granddad."

"See, now there is a good kid," Old Walt said.

The others nodded in agreement.

At first, I was excited to go with Granddad to eat the donuts and breakfast sandwiches. But after every visit, I knew there was much more in that small sun-filled room than donuts and coffee, and I couldn't wait for the next chance to go with Granddad and listen to these men tell stories and joke with each other. Something unexpected always happened.

CHAPTER 4

Sometimes It's Better to Stay Quiet

I remained between this world of solid matter and heaven. In my present state of weightlessness, I wasn't certain how much time had passed. There was no way to know. I felt as light as air as I looked down on myself in the operating room. My body down there didn't look so good.

And then I found myself back at the Donut Shop on another morning. The air felt crisp. Granddad and I, bundled in our jackets, were the first to arrive. It was unusual for us to be inside the shop before Parker. Parker liked to arrive first so he could pick out the seat that allowed him to listen to other people talking. His hearing wasn't as good as it once was, but he refused to wear his hearing aids. I wondered if his hearing had something to do with him being quiet all the time.

Parker was an interesting fellow. He was the most soft-spoken of the bunch. My grandfather told me Parker was a Marine in the Korean War and served two deployments there. He might have been a couple of years older than my grandfather but didn't look as old as the other men around the table. That was why the others called him Baby-faced Parker. His hair was oddly still dark and very thick. He had the type of skin that always was a light brown, even in the winter. I asked Granddad if Parker was someone from Mexico, but he said no. He said Parker was from Italy and had what is called olive skin.

Parker spoke with a slight accent. He listened more than he talked, but he never missed a chance to meet up with the others at the Donut Shop. I understood why he liked to go. I was like that, too. Any chance I had to tag along, I did.

On the Saturdays when I was with Granddad, I listened to all the guys as they told tall tales. They tried to see who could tell the most fascinating or most exaggerated or funniest story. Most of the time, I couldn't tell what was true and what was all in fun. Except for the war stories. I knew those were all true.

But Parker didn't tell as many stories as the others at the table. And Lawson told more stories than anyone, and his stories could last the whole morning.

Once, in the middle of one of Lawson's stories, Granddad said, "Lawson, take a breath so we can go eat lunch."

The rest of the bunch laughed, and it didn't seem to bother Lawson one bit. "What? You're buying our lunch?"

At that point, Old Walt saw the opportunity to leave, and he wasn't going to miss it. He stood up and headed for the door. Old Walt had been waiting for Lawson to wrap up his tall tale about the last time he went to the coast. Lawson's story started when he was in the driveway getting into the car to go on the trip, and by the time Granddad made his comment about lunch, Lawson's story had not yet made it halfway to his destination of South Padre Island. Lawson's stories never lacked details.

Parker, on the other hand, seldom started conversations. He observed everything and listened for a long time before he ever talked. One time, I noticed Parker didn't say a word for two solid hours. He sipped coffee and ate donuts the whole two hours before he uttered a word. Granddad said Parker's father taught him the benefits of being quiet and told him it would be important to stay quiet even as an adult. Granddad's comment puzzled me, so one morning before the others arrived, I asked him about it.

"Why was it important for Parker to learn to be quiet?"

"Wes, if I tell you that story, you can't ever, under any circumstances, mention it to Parker. He's not proud of what his dad did, but he understood why he did it."

Now I *had* to know. You don't tell a twelve-year-old something like "you can't ever under any circumstances talk about this" and think that same twelve-year-old will let that pass. I had to know.

"Well, young man? What do you say? Your word?"

"Yes sir." I nodded. I understood from Granddad's tone that what he was about to tell me was of great importance and, to show my maturity, I could never talk about this to anyone. I could never go back on my promise to him about anything. "I won't mention it."

"You see, Parker Robinson is not his real name."

Immediately, my brain worked on all the reasons why Parker changed his name. Did he or his dad do something awful? Maybe he had been in jail. Maybe his dad had been in trouble and had to run.

I looked Granddad in the eye with all the seriousness and maturity I could muster. I wanted to prove my trustworthiness to my grandfather. "What is his real name?"

Granddad paused, then it seemed he carefully chose his words. "Okay. I'm only telling this to you because you're my grandson and I want you to learn something from what happened to Parker. Understand?"

"Yes sir."

"His real name was Joseph Conigliaro."

"Joseph Conigliaro. That's certainly different from Parker Robinson. Why the name change?"

"This is all according to the story Parker told me years ago. Parker and his father came from Sicily somewhere around the late 1920s or early 1930s. A town called Palermo. I'm not sure of the date. And, the story goes, they were on an overcrowded small ship headed from Sicily to New York. People on the ship were coming to America for a better life. Some people traveled alone. Others with families. Some passengers were runaway criminals. But, to hear Parker tell it, all of them were very poor and very desperate.

"The ship was packed with passengers, and tempers were hot. Parker said the ship tossed and turned every which way in a severe storm. People got seasick. Some screamed for their very lives. Then, right in the middle of the ocean, at the height of the storm, some of the passengers got into a fight. Parker said some-one pulled a knife. People fell all over each other. He said he could see the knife shining as one man pulled it up and lunged toward another man. People were hurt, and since he was a little child, there was nothing he could do. He was afraid."

"That's awful."

"To hear Parker tell it, he was scared to death. He was only a little tyke, say maybe around four or five years old."

"No wonder he was frightened. I'd be afraid, too, being tossed around in a storm and having a fight break out right then."

"That's not all. A few people were wounded in the skirmish. One lady had a broken leg. Another person had a black eye and broken ribs. After a man was thrown overboard, Parker and his dad scuffled out of there to another spot on the deck."

"Yeah?"

"That was when Parker's dad spotted it."

"Spotted what? C'mon, tell me, please?"

Granddad knew how to drag out a story. Now I was more curious than ever, and he knew it. I could tell he stretched the story out on purpose because he grinned, knowing that reveal-ing only one detail at a time would drive me crazy. I wasn't very patient.

"They leaned against a wall on the deck. Parker's father reached down to grab Parker, and that was when he saw it."

I saw my middle-school self staring at Granddad who was all but laughing at my impatient face. He knew I couldn't take this suspense.

"There, on the deck, was a set of someone's papers."

"Papers? What kind of papers?"

"It was a set of identification papers to get into the United States. And the name Nick Robinson was on the top of the paper."

Here was the point where Granddad paused once again. He looked around the room to be sure no one was listening to him.

"Is that all to the story?"

"No. Of course, Parker, being just a young boy, didn't under-stand what happened or the significance of what was about to happen."

"What happened?"

"Parker's dad told Parker to be quiet, in Italian of course, and not to say a word or talk about the papers. His dad put the papers in his pocket. He didn't ask anyone about it or say anything about finding the papers. The next thing you know, Parker's dad heard the man thrown overboard was Nick Robinson."

"I see. So, Parker's father knew this Nick person wouldn't be asking about the papers."

"Yes. Nick Robinson was gone. Overboard. History. And now, Parker's father could use the papers to get into the country."

"Why didn't he want to use his own name, Conigliaro?"

"Parker's dad told Parker it would be easier to get a job and find a place to live if he had a more American-sounding name. Parker said his father made him repeat his new name, Parker Robinson, all day long for days."

At this point, Jae interrupted our conversation and set our plates of donuts on the table and poured us cups of coffee.

"You two so chatty this morning."

Granddad cleared his throat and said, "Good morning to you, too, Jae."

She laughed. "No worry. I bring your milk, Wes." She winked and turned toward the milk sitting on the counter. "The others are late. Car trouble."

"Oh?"

"Yes. Jimmy had to get Walt and Parker. Parker go with Walt and truck broke down. Jimmy went to help. Jimmy called and told me, 'Tell that old Marine not to eat all the donuts.'"

Granddad laughed. "Where's Lawson?"

Jae shrugged her shoulders. "I not his mother. Don't ask me." Jae waved her hand to dismiss the question and scurried back to the counter.

At that exact moment, Lawson walked through the door. Granddad yelled loud enough to get Lawson's attention, "Jae, you'd have to be about a hundred and fifty years old to be old enough to be Lawson's mother."

Lawson looked completely bewildered.

Granddad laughed and Lawson smiled as he took his seat.

"Late getting out of bed?" Granddad asked.

"No, no. I was on the phone with the plumber. Think I have a broken or leaking pipe on the side of the house."

"Everything is breaking this morning. Walt's truck, your pipe—"

"Well, everything else is working just fine, and looking good as new. Thank you." Lawson laughed, winked, and straightened up as if to be ready to catch the eye of a lady.

"Who are you expecting now?" Granddad laughed.

"I'm not telling you. You'd never let me hear the end of it."

Granddad egged him on. "Come on. You know I will find out soon enough."

"Not unless you are going to the church bake sale in an hour." Then, without saying another word, Lawson stood up, went to the counter, and picked out his donuts.

"Granddad, tell me what you meant about Parker. You said Parker understood why his dad took the papers and the other man's name."

"You see, Wes, there is no other country like ours in the entire world. During the time Parker came to the United States, the world was in a depression and times were hard. People couldn't eat. No one had jobs. People were homeless and waiting in food lines. Parker's father wanted to take care of him. Parker's mother died from an illness, so it was up to his father to raise him. Parker's father found steady work here in the United States. After they came to America, they had a good life, food to eat, and a small home. They became citizens as soon as they were able. And when Parker was old enough, he joined the Marines. Said he would die if needed to save this country. He said this country saved him and his father and it was the best country in the entire world."

My eyes were fixed on my grandfather's face. I felt the intensity of his words and saw how important this was in his eyes.

"Do you understand?"

I nodded.

"Always remember how blessed we are to live here. Never take that for granted. Ever."

"Yes sir."

CHAPTER FIVE

The Great Heist

Lawson returned to the table with his plate full of donuts and took a seat.

"Okay, Lawson, tell us. Who are you going to meet? Her name? You know, at the church bake sale?" Granddad asked him again.

"Not telling."

"Okay. Since you won't say, I'll guess. Let's see, it has to be Ethel down at the bank."

Lawson laughed. "Shoot, no. If I had someone like Ethel and all that money, I wouldn't be hanging out with the likes of you. I'd be down at the country club."

"Maribel? At the drugstore? You know, attractive, brown hair. She helps people with their pictures, cameras, and stuff."

Lawson was silent.

Granddad continued. "You know who I'm talking about. Maribel. Always talking with the men in the store."

Lawson's face turned an interesting shade of red.

"Ah-ha! That's it! Maribel! She's a looker," Granddad laughed.

Lawson grumbled, "Don't be lookin' at her."

"Why? Are you two a thing now?"

"Not sayin'."

These two would have gone on all day if Parker, Walt, and Jimmy hadn't finally arrived and opened the Donut Shop door.

Lawson seized the opportunity to change the conversation. "Look, it's the three stooges."

"Funny," Walt said.

"It wasn't funny," Jimmy said. "I had to go pick up these two knuckleheads down the road. Broken down truck."

Granddad noted, "Everything is breaking today. First, Lawson's pipe and now Walt's truck."

"Did you do it?" Jimmy asked Granddad.

"Do what?"

"Eat all the donuts? Didn't Jae tell you I called?"

"She did, but it was too late. I'd already eaten them all." Granddad leaned back in his chair and patted his stomach.

Jae heard the conversation and yelled from the counter, "No, there's plenty. You come order."

Once Walt, Jimmy, and Parker entered the shop, the conversation changed. But I learned a lesson about how things used to be. It was a lesson I wished my history teacher had talked about. My history books and the lectures I had in the past were not even close to being as interesting as the stories these men told me. The story about Parker, or Joseph Conigliaro, was a lesson about people looking for help in our great country and how it used to be in the past for immigrants from Europe. That story opened my eyes to the great lengths people go to in order to come to the United States.

Jimmy, Walt, and Parker took their seats, and Jae poured more coffee for everyone. It was at that precise moment the warmth and quiet of our typical Saturday Donut Shop gathering was interrupted. I didn't recognize the man, dressed in a shirt, jeans, and cowboy hat, who bolted through the door.

"Call the police!" The man bent over to catch his breath. "Some people a couple of doors down at the Central Store are threatening the store owner. They're yelling and carrying on. Taking stuff out of the store. Just taking it right out of there without paying for it. Look out the window!"

We all scrambled to the window the fastest a bunch of older men and a kid could do. We watched two men run out of the store with their arms loaded down with all kinds of things. They ran down the street, struggling with the stolen goods.

Granddad pointed at the men. "Don't recognize them."

Lawson agreed. "Not from around here."

Jae, panicked, reached for the phone and called the police. She reported everything the man who burst into the shop said.

We watched the two thieves disappear from view and then resumed our breakfast.

Lawson shook his head. "Boy, I miss the good old days. People didn't invade a store in the middle of the day. What has happened to this world? People are just plain crazy." He took another bite of his cinnamon donut.

The other old guys only nodded in agreement. They couldn't say anything because, at that moment, their mouths were all stuffed full of donuts.

"Tell me about what it was like. How did it used to be?" I asked Lawson.

"Son, it was peaceful. At least it was in my town. People talked to each other instead of going crazy. A person would ask a question, politely, instead of charging into a store and yelling. Or worse, breaking windows out and taking things. Unbelievable," he said.

"How are things different now?" I asked.

With his mouth half full of a bear claw, Granddad said, "No respect. People don't respect each other. They are only thinking about themselves."

"Yes sir." Lawson agreed. "Back in the day, if someone had a gripe or a question, they just came peacefully into the sheriff's office and asked me. There was none of this charging into places, breaking down doors and windows, taking things right out of the store in broad daylight. And it isn't just people these intruders don't respect. They don't respect property. They don't care if you and I work hard to buy our own TV or car or whatever. Nowadays, some people just do whatever they want. They wanted to take that stuff from the store because they wanted it. It's unbelievable. In the early days, people helped each other take care of things. They'd help with each other's yards, help with repairs, because they were neighbors and lived in the same community. People were polite and respectful."

"Tell us, Lawson," Jimmy said, "How would you have han-

29

dled this, you know, when you were sheriff?"

"If this had just happened? This invasion and theft? My deputies would have brought those scoundrels right downtown, and we would have arrested them."

Lawson had no sooner finished telling his strategy as a former sheriff when Pete, the local policeman on patrol, pushed open the shop door. "Hi fellas, I saw your trucks in the parking lot and thought you might help me out. Did y'all see anything going on down the street?"

Granddad was the first to answer. "Yes sir, Pete."

"Can you recall any details?"

My grandfather hesitated and replied, "Just a couple of fellas who weren't from around here."

Officer Pete looked at Lawson and said, "Lawson, you know how to make these observations. What can you tell me?"

Lawson swallowed his coffee before replying. "Two males, probably late teens or early twenties. One about six feet tall, the other fella shorter, maybe five feet eight or ten. Both had black hair. One possibly Hispanic. The shorter fella had a tattoo on his face. Both wearing sweatshirts. Tall one, black sweatshirt. Smaller one had on a camouflage hoodie and might be mistaken as a hunter, but he was just hunting merchandise."

Officer Pete chuckled. "You're probably right about that. Haven't seen too many hunters in these parts with tattooed faces. Can you think of anything else? Were they on foot?"

"Yes sir. But they were headed down the street where there's parking behind the main buildings."

"Thank you." Pete pushed his radio on and said, "Officer Pete here, on that 10-31 at Central Store. Send officer behind Main Street stores. Two male suspects on foot. One in camo sweatshirt, other black sweatshirt."

Officer Pete's cellphone buzzed. We all listened intently to Officer Pete's side of the conversation. "Yes...Thank you, Shirley... I will be right down to pick them up...Yes, any other witnesses call in?...I see. Thank you."

The officer hung up and turned to us. "Shirley just got a

couple of pictures faxed in. Now, she can't use technology all that well to send the pictures out here. I'm gonna run over and pick them up. Can you fellas hang around until I get back? I want to see if these are the guys you saw."

"Be happy to," Lawson said.

"I'm never one to mind staying at the Donut Shop longer than I planned," Jimmy said.

Old Walt agreed. "I know what you mean. I think I can find room for a couple more donut holes."

Officer Pete left, and Jae poured refills into our coffee cups.

"Besides," Old Walt said, "I need to talk with Pete about my fence."

Granddad asked, "Something wrong with your fence?"

"Yep. It's cut."

Jimmy couldn't resist. "Why would you cut your fence?"

"Didn't. But, if these two fellas are traveling on foot, they might have done it."

"Good point," Granddad agreed.

We enjoyed our additional donuts, chatted, and waited for Pete, who soon returned with papers in his hand.

"Now, fellas, here are several guys on the run between here and Mexico. Shirley found ten photos of possible suspects from surrounding counties." He laid the faxed pictures on the table. "Any of these men look familiar?"

Without any hesitation, Lawson said, "This one here, and... that one. That's the shorter one with the tattoo."

"No doubt?"

Lawson shook his head. "No sir. That's them."

The others passed around the pictures and agreed.

"Thanks, fellas."

Old Walt said, "Hey, Pete, I wanted to run something by you. I had my fence cut yesterday. I noticed it because a cow got out last night. Any chance these two might have done it?"

"Possible. Tell you what, I'll be out to your place this afternoon and look around. You'll be home later?"

"Yep."

"Okay. I'll be by after lunch. Say, did you get the cow squared away?"

"Yep. Sure did."

"Good. See you in a couple of hours."

CHAPTER SIX

Undercover Operations

After Officer Pete left, my heart at last settled down to its usual relaxed Saturday pace as we all took our seats around the table once again. Jae came back around with another plate of donut holes, and she filled our coffee cups again.

"The Central Store heist is about the most excitement we've had in these parts in a while," Lawson said. "This town is usually as laid back as my town in Virginia. Once the '70s ended, things were pretty quiet in my town."

This prompted Jimmy to ask, "What was the most exciting time you had when you were sheriff?"

"I suppose the '60s."

I turned to Lawson and hoped he would tell me another story about his days as sheriff.

Old Walt cleared his throat, patted me on the back, and said, "Tell the boy about the riots."

"Riots?" Lawson asked.

"Yep. The riots."

"We didn't have any riots in my town back when I was sheriff."

Old Walt smiled and said, "That's what I mean. Tell him why you didn't have any riots in the old days in Virginia."

"Well, we were supposed to have riots."

"Supposed to?" I asked.

"When I was sheriff during the '60s, the country had some challenging things going on. There was unrest, Civil Rights movements, beginnings of the Vietnam War. And all over the country,

33

there were organized and mostly peaceful Civil Rights marches. Dr. King was very popular. Everyone loved him. Me too. He knew how to get people to listen and understand the right way. Loved his message. Still do. I believe he had the right idea. But not everyone agreed."

"What do you mean?" I asked. "People disagreed about being peaceful?"

"Yep. And it was not only the people against the Civil Rights movement who disagreed with a peaceful protest approach, but some people within the movement disagreed as well. You see, there were a lot of people, and I mean a lot, who wanted to force their way on other people. Force their beliefs on people. Like now. No talking nowadays. Just people wanting to have things their way. The people smashing into the store don't care what others think or believe."

"Get to the point, Lawson," Jimmy interrupted. "The boy doesn't have all day to be waiting for the rest of the story."

"Okay. As I was saying, there were people on both sides who thought violence was the answer. And people on both sides who didn't want violence. Now, Dr. King didn't believe violence was the way. He wanted the marches and protests to be peaceful. And so did I."

Lawson paused to drink of his coffee.

"Well, go on," Granddad said. "Tell him what you did."

"You see, Wes, I had some…what you might call undercover people. Kind of like spies. No one knew they were working for me. They infiltrated both sides, and then they would come back to the office and report to me."

I nodded, hanging on to every word.

"So, I found out from these undercover fellows there were some outsiders, people not from my little town in Virginia were involved. They were coming in from everywhere. Many of these protesters came from out of state. In fact, these troublemakers traveled all over the south looking for a march, a riot, or protest to attend, just so they could stir things up. Well, they were planning on coming to town, and Dr. King and his people had already arranged to have a peaceful march down Main Street. Dr. King didn't want these outsiders coming in to ruin things."

"What did you do? If you knew they were coming, how did you stop it?"

"Well, son, I put out a call to every man I knew and asked as many as were able to come downtown. I brought them into the town hall. I told them we had some troublemakers wanting to come into our little town. I explained Dr. King's beliefs and his wishes for a peaceful event. I asked them if they wanted to be deputized to help me out and to keep our town safe. Then I deputized them right then and there on the spot. I told each one where to stand on the street where the march was to take place. On the day of the march, it looked like our police force was huge."

From where I was floating in time and space, looking down on my twelve-year-old self, I could see my enormous eyes as the younger version of me listened.

"I sent my regular deputies, the state troopers, and others I borrowed from a few towns around, out to the highways. They were told to stop any outsiders and turn them around. We only had two roads coming into town and it didn't take much manpower to put up a couple of roadblocks and ask strangers for their license to see where they were coming from and where they were going and why."

"Did it work?" I asked.

"Yep. I called Dr. King's group and told them we would protect them when they came in. They could sit in the road or do whatever they wanted to do that day. But no outsiders were allowed. And I knew Dr. King's group would be peaceful. That was the way he wanted it."

"What happened?"

"The peaceful protesters came into town and sat right in the road. Others sat on the large steps going up to the courthouse. Some sang, some prayed, some peacefully chanted. It lasted for most of the afternoon. The march went off as smooth as silk. No problem. You know why?"

"Because you had a lot of men out there?"

"Any stranger who came to town thought we had a large police force. That was part of it. But the other part was Dr. King and the people coming to march peacefully respected us and we respected them. Respect. Just like your grandfather said, respect. I tell you, that's what is missing today."

Jae brought more coffee and filled our cups once more. "Oh, so serious. No chuckles today?"

"Jae," Grandad said in a loud whisper, "Look at Lawson's face."

"What's wrong?" Lawson scrunched his eyebrows together. "Do I have sugar on my nose or something?"

"Just right there." Granddad gestured, but of course, Lawson had nothing on his face.

Lawson wiped his nose with a napkin. "Did I get it?"

Jimmy laughed. "No, now you moved it right there on your cheek."

Laughter broke out around the table. By now, Lawson had figured out there was nothing on his face. He shook his finger at my grandfather. "You just wait! I will get you back."

Granddad laughed and said, "You just don't want Maribel to see you with sugar on your nose."

Jimmy asked, "What's this? He's sweet on Maribel?"

Now Lawson's face turned red. "I was trying to keep it quiet."

The table erupted with laughter once again. These men knew how to enjoy each other and life in general.

I was jolted again and found myself back above the surgical table. Somehow, I had remembered the bits and pieces of the stories, jokes, and conversations that took place in the Donut Shop. But reliving them was something I never would have imagined. Being in that place and time again meant more to me now than it did years ago.

My body looked weak and pale. I wondered if I would have more of my own life to live and enjoy. Would the surgery be successful? Would I be able to go home and enjoy the rest of my life? If I made it, I wouldn't take one second for granted.

CHAPTER SEVEN

Old Walt's Fence

This was getting old. I had heard of people having these near-death experiences, but nothing I'd heard or read ever indicated how long one might be in this state of in-between-ness. In this state, I felt no pain. I figured my body was sensing pain, but after all, I wasn't in my body to feel the pain. The only sensations I was aware of were floating, weightlessness, moving around in the air, some smells, and sounds. Somehow, wherever my body went, I was above it. I could hear people talking, lights buzzing, the clinking of instruments, and the beeping of equipment. Questions still haunted me. What happened? Why am I here? And of course, would I make it? Would I live or be taken to heaven?

Once again, as quickly as I'd been jolted away from the Donut Shop, my mind returned to that earlier year with Granddad.

The talk of the town for the next few days was about the heist of items from the Central Store. I was not surprised when Granddad and I sat down at our table that the talk was about more details and rumors circulating in town.

Parker, who was usually quiet, seemed to be very excited about the news of the morning. "Did you hear? Federal agents are here."

"Oh?" Jimmy asked.

Parker continued. "I heard it from Jae. They called and said they're coming to the Donut Shop."

At this news, Lawson sat up and called out to Jae. "Say, those federal officers coming by here, Jae?"

"Yes. They call. Want to speak to Old Walt."

This got Old Walt's attention. "I didn't do it!"

"No, old man." Jae laughed. "They say they want to ask you about fence."

"They didn't want to ask Officer Pete?" Old Walt asked.

"No. They ask him already. He coming, too. Be here soon."

This was shaping up to be an entertaining morning. Nothing could beat a pile of delicious donuts, hot coffee, and federal agents. How often did a kid like me meet real federal agents?

"Say, youngster," Old Walt said, "You look like you need a few more donut holes this morning to get you ready for the day. You need more energy."

He knew I wouldn't refuse. I had just piled a couple more on my plate when the door opened. In came Officer Pete, one man dressed in a dark green uniform and another man dressed in a light brown shirt and dark brown pants.

"Good morning," Officer Pete said to Jae. He walked toward our table.

"Fellas, this is Carlos," he gestured toward the man in the dark green shirt. "He is from the Border Patrol, and this is Jake, a State Trooper. They wanted to speak to you about what happened the other day. You know, the two men who stole the property from the Central Store. And they want to ask you, Walter, about your fence."

"Good morning. As Pete said, I am Officer Carlos Martinez, and this is Officer Jake Walton. We work this county and the surrounding counties. Officer Pete reported the cuttings of your fence, Walter. He said you've had your fence cut several times in the past and no one is ever found."

"Nice to meet you fellas," Old Walt said. "Uh, yes, I've had the fence cut many times. It's been happening more frequently lately."

Carlos nodded. "And you've never seen anyone coming through?"

"No sir."

Jake spoke up. "These two, I believe you all identified them?" He placed two pictures on our table.

We all nodded yes.

"These two," Carlos pointed to the pictures, "we suspect have committed several robberies, usually related to drugs and such. But this fella here." He pointed to the picture of the man with the tattoo on his face. "He is believed to be a gang member of the MS-13 gang. He is armed and assumed dangerous. He's been accused of assaulting an officer with a knife, resisting arrest, and punching another officer. So, you all look out for him. If you see him again or hear of anyone who might fit the description, call us or Officer Pete right away. And don't try to deal with them yourselves."

"We'll try not to, but old habits die hard," Old Walt said.

"Old habits? Military or law enforcement?" Carlos asked. At this, everyone around the table laughed and nodded.

"Both," Lawson said.

"Marines?" Carlos asked.

Three nods by the Marines.

"One Navy here and retired sheriff," Lawson said.

Jimmy raised his hand. "One Army."

"Okay. I know how you fellas might think. And I know you want to help by taking matters into your own hands. But for these two scoundrels, you let us handle them. Understood?"

We all nodded again.

Border Patrol Agent Carlos asked, "Now, Walter, have you found anything unusual on your property? Items that weren't yours?"

"Yes sir. I've found clothes. You know, a torn shirt or a shoe, from time to time. And trash. Somehow, these trespassers always seem to leave trash behind."

"Any evidence of campfires? Or any drug-related items?"

"No sir. Not that I'm aware of."

Jake nodded and said, "That's good. Looks like they don't stay on your property long. The bad news is, they are just passing through to go somewhere else and get into trouble."

Carlos handed us each a card. "You see anything, you let us know."

Granddad said, "Will do."

"Yes sir, and thank you all for your service," Lawson added. "Buy you fellas some breakfast?"

Jake shook his head. "No, thank you. We ate earlier. Rain check?"

"Sure thing," Lawson replied. "Come back by any morning. We're usually here."

Officer Pete said, "Well, thanks, fellas. We will be in touch."

The donut eating continued, and Jae brought another round of coffee and donut holes. "You see two men they looking for?"

Granddad said, "Not since the other day when they ran out of the Central Store."

"Me either," Jae said, adding more coffee to my cup. "Police should catch them soon. Don't want them coming in here."

"Now, Jae, they might show up to grab some of these donuts! They heard how delicious your donuts are all the way to Mexico," Jimmy said.

"No, silly. Don't want them to take my money," Jae replied.

"Ah, we wouldn't let them do that," Granddad said.

Jimmy turned to Old Walt and said, "Say, you know what you need at your place, Old Walt?"

"Nope. Tell me."

"You need someone at your ranch like you used to have. What was that fella's name?"

Granddad replied, "You are thinking about Rodrigo. I remember him."

Old Walt nodded. "Yes, good old Rodrigo. He was the best ranch hand I ever had. He worked the cattle, kept the other ranch hands in line, and took care of the property. Mended fences. Repaired the barn. And he guarded the property better than a policeman would have. You never knew him, did you, Wes?"

"No sir."

"He was something else. He lived in the little house on the west of my property. You know, it's close to the highway."

"That's right, that little brick house off the main road going out of town," Parker said. "I liked good old Rodrigo."

"Only problem was," Old Walt continued, "he thought he had more authority than anyone on the property, including me, the state troopers, and the police. And Rodrigo," Old Walt laughed, "He would stand out on the highway if he heard a car or truck coming by too fast. He would yell at them to slow down. He'd go right out onto the road and yell. Sometimes the cars would slow down, but more times than not, they honked at him, yelled back, and even threatened him a time or two. I was afraid he was gonna get beat up or run over someday."

Jimmy asked, "What ever happened to Rodrigo? He was here for years, and then one day, he wasn't."

"Well, you see, he worked on the ranch most months of the year. But in the coldest part of winter, he would go back home to Mexico. Said it was warmer there and he'd go visit his family and to the beach by Veracruz, Mexico, December through the first week of February. Then he'd come back up here to work. He made sure the part-time workers knew what to do while he was away. Then, one winter, he went home and didn't come back.

"I tried for years to locate him and find out what happened. I decided he'd gotten sick or died. But one day, I received a letter from him. He'd become a grandfather and decided to stay in Mexico with his family. A good guy. I miss having him around. These trespassers wouldn't have made it on my property if Rodrigo were still here."

"Yep," Granddad said, "He was a wonderful worker. I know that for sure. He would help me out occasionally."

"I remember he helped you with that leak you had in your kitchen ceiling," Parker added.

Granddad nodded. "Yes, he had a lot of good skills."

A sharp sound got my attention, and I looked down at my lifeless body. The doctor and nurses were moving frantically, as if something bad had happened. They reminded me of ants running to their anthill. They weren't talking, just shouting frantic requests for instruments and yelling orders of what needed to be done.

CHAPTER EIGHT

Ranch Stories, Hamburgers, and Dynamite

I merely blinked, and I was jerked from above the operating room table back to years ago in the middle of the same conversation. I was still sitting at the table with Granddad and his coffee shop buddies.

"Old Rodrigo. I sure missed him when he was away in the winter. But when he returned that February, he helped me during one of the worst winter storms we ever had. Dangerous times on the ranch during the winter."

"What happens in the winter?" I asked.

"Wes, when it is super cold, and we have had a hard freeze, the could cattle die. It is cold for them, too. And Rodrigo, he knew all kinds of ways to prevent the cattle from freezing. The babies, the smaller cattle, they would be the most vulnerable."

"What would Rodrigo do?"

"Here, in Texas, our cattle might not grow as thick of hair in the winter as cattle up north, because, well, we don't have that long of a cold season. Rodrigo would build us some wind breaks where the cattle liked to hang out. He used the tall cedars and added more brush and wood to make the break in the open fields. The cattle would gather there in spots, together, in a huddle, and help keep each other warm. He made sure they had water, which meant going out and breaking up the ice on the ponds. Trouble was, if it was really cold, the ponds would freeze right back up!"

"I'd never thought about that."

Old Walt laughed. "Yes, Wes, a lot of care goes into getting those hamburgers on the tables."

I smiled.

Old Walt continued, "Now, Rodrigo would go check on the babies. Sometimes, he took extra hay bales out and made beds to keep the babies warmer."

"Isn't there any place the cattle can go?" I asked.

"On a ranch with a smaller herd, yes. You can build sheds or have some go into a large barn and others gather around the barn. But, well, I have too many cattle, I suppose."

"Do any of the cattle ever..."

"Die?"

"Yes sir. Did you lose any?"

"Yes. From time to time. A baby or smaller cow. Sometimes a full-grown cow out of shape or left out in the elements too long without food or water—"

Jimmy interrupted, "But what about the time you lost thirteen?"

Old Walt shook his head. "Still upsets me, Jimmy." He paused for a moment and continued, "That wasn't from the cold. It was lightning."

"Thirteen cows? What happened?" I was intrigued.

"You see, Wes, the cattle were under a tree. They do that, collect under trees. Lightning struck the tree and went all the way down through the roots and the very ground the cattle were standing on. Lost every one of them under that tree. It was a sad day to go out there and move all those dead cattle. A sad day."

"I hate to ask, but what did you do with them?"

"Had to dig a pit. All of them. In the pit," Old Walt shook his head. "Rodrigo and I spent the better part of three days getting all the cattle buried."

"Just read about a lot of cattle frozen up in North Dakota last year. Over a thousand on one ranch. Ranching is difficult in bad weather," Granddad said.

Old Walt added, "It sure was difficult for me and Rodrigo that year in that lightning storm."

"Did you hear about those cows in that tornado last year?" Parker asked.

"Yes, I heard about that one, too," Granddad said.

I hadn't. I shook my head no.

"Said they were mostly battered by debris, but a couple were found miles from their ranch," Parker replied.

"Guess I'd never thought about what cattle do in storms."

Jimmy laughed. "Might have been worse for that chicken farmer up there in the north part of the county. Blew away the chicken coop. I heard he lost over a thousand chickens in that storm. And the chicken poop was everywhere for miles around."

Old Walt laughed and said, "It is tough for the farmer to get those fried chicken wings to the table, too, Wes."

"Farming and ranching seem like hard work," I said.

"Tough work, son," Granddad said.

"And can be dangerous," Lawson added.

Jimmy laughed. "This from the man who boxed a gorilla!"

The men laughed.

"Now," Jimmy continued, "Speaking of dangerous, tell Wes about the engagement ring."

"What?" Lawson looked puzzled. "There wasn't anything dangerous about the engagement ring."

"Not the ring, you old squid. How you got it."

"Oh, that is another story that happened out on a farm. It was a dairy farm—"

"See, cows are dangerous." Jimmy laughed.

"Anyway, I needed some money so—"

"Let me guess, you wanted to box some big guy for money or maybe a dairy cow?" Granddad laughed.

"No, no. I was out at old Jesse's dairy farm with a friend of mine. And Jesse needed a well. My friend and I had been digging and digging. We weren't making much headway. We hit a level of mud and rock, and we just couldn't get it to go any deeper with our shovels."

"What did you do?" I asked.

"I had heard another friend of mine over on the other side of town might have an answer. He was someone who had experience with well-digging. I got in my truck and headed over there. He had a solution all right."

"Get to the point," Granddad said, "My coffee is getting cold."

"Okay, so my friend over there on the other side of town said he used explosives. Now, I thought that was all well and good except for one tiny detail."

No one said a word. We knew Lawson had the stage and he loved it. We also knew he loved watching us as we waited for the end of the story.

"You see, this friend of mine, well, he wasn't exactly trained in explosives. He had some experience in the military, but he wasn't really trained. Right up front, he said he didn't know what he was doing, and he wasn't sure it would work. The main thing he kept repeating was 'as soon as you light this, run for cover and get as far away as possible.'"

"Light it? What was it?" I asked.

"Dynamite."

My eyes bugged out. "Dynamite? Had he put the thing together himself?"

"Yes. He made his own explosives back in the day. I went back to the well, and all I kept thinking about was the money the farmer would pay me to get the well in so his dairy cows would have another water supply. And if I earned that money, that ring I saw in the jewelry store window downtown would be on my sweetheart's finger."

"Well, you must have made it out okay," Jimmy said.

"What do you mean?" Lawson asked.

"Cause you're sittin' here."

After the laughter died down, Lawson continued. "I made it out, but just barely. I climbed down as low as I could, as far as we were able to dig. I put the dynamite down, struck the match, then lit the fuse. The fuse started burning. I began my climb out, but my foot slipped. The mud down there was slippery. I scrambled and yelled. My buddy who was helping me threw me a rope, and I hightailed it out of there as fast as I could. As soon as I climbed out of the well and ran a few yards, I heard the explosion."

"Wow! Just in time," I said.

"Yep. The mud flew out of the well and all over both of us! But I got my money! After I went home and showered, I went straight down to the jewelry store and bought that ring I'd seen in the window."

"She must have been something else," I said.

"She was, Wes. She was. I hope someday you can find someone like my sweet Betty Lou."

The beeping monitors took me back to the operating room. I wondered if I would ever get out of this room full of equipment and doctors and nurses all dressed in blue scrubs from head to toe. I wondered if my parents were still okay and where they were in the hospital.

CHAPTER NINE

Cold Morning in December

Although I still floated above the surgeon and nurses frantically working on my body on the operating table, suddenly I felt cold. I felt chilled to my bones. It was the first time I had felt anything since I'd been floating up here. It scared me. I didn't know if feeling temperature was a good or bad sign. Even my insides were cold. Maybe it meant I was getting sensation back. On the other hand, I'd heard people feel cold right before they die.

Shivering and not sure if I was coming back into my body or if I was in the process of leaving the earth at last, my mind drifted back to one cold morning. I was with Granddad on a Saturday. Rather than heading straight to the Donut Shop, he turned the car a different direction. He drove along a meandering road headed away from town.

"Where are we going?"

"Well, Wes, today is a very important day. I wanted to show you something and tell you about it before we head to the Donut Shop."

Not knowing where we were going, I kept quiet and wondered what Granddad had planned. I glanced out at the pasture where longhorn steers grazed. This was not our typical route, and Granddad was not his typical cheerful self. He was unusually quiet and serious today.

Granddad parked the car in a small parking lot in front of an open gate with fancy swirling ironwork across the top of the entryway. The walls on each side were made of limestone. Above the open gate, the writing said, "Memorial Park." *Is Granddad taking me to a graveyard?* In the past, he had taken me to visit Grandma's gravesite, but that was at another cemetery on the older side of town.

Granddad didn't say a word when he got out of the car. I followed him up the small stone sidewalk. It was pristine. Not even weeds were brave enough to grow between the cracks of the walkway. The grass was landscaped to perfection.

Once inside the limestone walls, there were no graves, just large stone markers with bronze plaques. Each plaque had names and pictures engraved on it. There were so many American flags flying around in the small park that it exploded with the colors red, white, and blue. Three words rolled over and over in my mind: reverent, majestic, magnificent. This place was about the most impressive place I'd seen.

"This is a tribute, Wes. This is a memorial to all the men and women who gave their lives defending our great country. Some of these young people who died were only a few years older than you are now when they left home to join the military service. They went into war because they believed in our country. They didn't want anyone to take away our freedom or change our country."

I watched as Granddad walked over to the plaque about the Korean War. He touched the stone, ran his finger over the writing, and stood silent. After a few moments, he said, "Brave men who died beside me."

For a brief second, I noticed a lone tear making its way down his cheek. He quietly brushed the tear away and said nothing more.

We walked from one stone to another and read about each war, each conflict. Then he stopped at one of the larger stones. "You know today's date?"

I replied, "Uh, the seventh of December."

He read the plaque aloud. "December 7, 1941. Two-thousand three-hundred thirty-three servicemen died in the attack on Pearl Harbor." He paused for a moment. "Today is the anniversary of the attack on Pearl Harbor."

We stood in silence. I sensed he was thinking back about the war he was in and the wars before the Korean War. After some time, he said, "You know, Wes, I was only nine years old when I heard President Roosevelt make his speech about Pearl Harbor. I listened to it on the small radio in the family room with my parents. No television then, and no internet. We got a newspaper, but not until a couple of days after the attack. In fact, Roosevelt's speech was the day after the attack and the newspaper came later the next day. It took time to get the news to Washington, DC, and time to figure out what happened. Communication wasn't instant back then."

Not knowing what to say, I only listened. The sun warmed the air. We were silent for at least ten minutes until Granddad glanced at his watch and said, "Better go get some breakfast."

The ride back to town was quiet, and Granddad had that look about him, as if he were in church listening to a Higher Power. I knew Granddad's mind was elsewhere. I sensed he had so much more to say about this historic date. Maybe it was too difficult to talk about, or there was something important he wanted to tell me but wasn't ready. I hoped Granddad would mention the date to the group sitting around the wooden table at the Donut Shop.

We entered the shop and found Parker, Jimmy, Lawson, and Old Walt sitting with their plates and coffee cups full. When they saw Granddad, all saluted each other silently. It was an unspoken code that told me in an instant they were all thinking about the importance of this day.

"I see you brought this young whippersnapper back around," Jimmy said.

"Don't you ever feed that boy? He looks pretty skinny." Old Walt laughed.

I smiled because I knew Old Walt was going to offer me extra donut holes. He always did, and I always took them. I didn't want to be rude or anything.

"Go by the memorial already?" Lawson asked.

"Yes sir," Granddad said. "I told Wes about the day of the attack and reminded him you were in the war, Lawson."

Lawson nodded. "Yep. I sure was. But I didn't join until the end of the war. I was fifteen when Japan attacked Pearl Harbor."

I listened to Granddad and Lawson as they took turns recalling what they heard on that fateful day, the day after the attack on Pearl Harbor. They talked about what they had learned during the speech and in the news and their feelings about the horrific attack.

"I remember it so well," Granddad said, "the day after the attack. I sat with my family and a couple of neighbors in the living room around the radio and heard President Roosevelt say, 'Yesterday, December 7, 1941, a date which will live in infamy, the United States of America was suddenly and deliberately attacked by naval and air forces of the Empire of Japan.'"

Lawson nodded. "Yes, the President explained the situation throughout his speech. It was a very comprehensive speech. Roosevelt summed up the thinking of the military and the President. I remember Roosevelt said, 'The United States was at peace with that Nation and, at the solicitation of Japan, was still in conversation with its Government and its Emperor looking toward the maintenance of peace in the Pacific.'" Then Lawson reached into his pocket and took out an old newspaper clipping. He found a place on the page and pointed to the line as he read, "Then Roosevelt said, 'Indeed, one hour after Japanese air squadrons had commenced bombing in the American Island of Oahu, the Japanese Ambassador to the United States and his colleague delivered to our Secretary of State a formal reply to a recent American message. And while this reply stated that it seemed useless to continue the existing diplomatic negotiations, it contained no threat or hint of war or of armed attack.'

"It was hard for us, as a country," Lawson continued, "To believe Japan carried out this attack at the same time our countries were in discussions together. Did you know, Wes, the United States and Japan were supposed to be having what were called 'peaceful negotiations' at that very same time? It was unbelievable to us. The entire country was in disbelief."

Granddad shook his head, as if he still didn't understand why the attack happened. "Wes, President Roosevelt explained the reason our country knew it was an unprovoked attack. In his speech, he told us all that America was deliberately attacked. Roosevelt said, 'It will be recorded that the distance of Hawaii from Japan makes it obvious that the attack was deliberately planned many days or even weeks ago. During the intervening time, the Japanese Government has deliberately sought to deceive the United States by false statements and expressions of hope for continued peace.' So, he wanted the world to know, and Japan to know, that we knew Japan planned it ahead of time. He reminded the American people of the distance of the attack, and this was an indication that the attack happened on purpose...it was planned well in advance."

Then Lawson said, "Most people don't realize how close the military forces of Japan were to our homeland at that time. Most people today think Japan was fighting us only near Hawaii. But Roosevelt went on to say, 'The attack yesterday on the Hawaiian Islands has caused severe damage to American naval and military forces. I regret to tell you that very many American lives have been lost. In addition, American ships have been reported torpedoed on the high seas between San Francisco and Honolulu.'"

"Really? All the way to the coast of the United States?"

"Yes," Lawson replied.

Granddad added, "And until Roosevelt's speech, we didn't know how many places Japan attacked at the same time. The President listed each attack for the American people, and Congress, to fully understand what our country was facing. He wanted to let us know how broad this attack was and that it involved places other than Hawaii. So, he told us all the places that were attacked. Roosevelt said, 'Yesterday the Japanese Government also launched an attack against Malaya. Last night Japanese forces attacked Hong Kong. Last night Japanese forces attacked Guam. Last night Japanese forces attacked the Philippine Islands. Last night the Japanese attacked Wake Island. And this morning the Japanese attacked Midway Island.'"

"So, the attack was widespread," I nodded with understanding. "Did Roosevelt say anything else?"

Granddad nodded his head to note that it was not the end of Roosevelt's speech. He continued, "Roosevelt kind of summed it up by saying, 'Japan has, therefore, undertaken a surprise offensive extending throughout the Pacific area. The facts of yesterday and today speak for themselves. The people of the United States have already formed their opinions and well understand the implications to the very life and safety of our Nation.'"

Lawson said, "The President didn't waste any time, either. Roosevelt got back to business. He said, 'As Commander in Chief of the Army and Navy, I have directed that all measures be taken for our defense. But always will our whole Nation remember the character of the onslaught against us.'"

"Wow," I said, "Roosevelt addressed the attack right away."

Granddad nodded. "Yes, he did. His speech was powerful. Hearing of the events that happened on December seventh, the whole country pulled together to show strength. His speech that day had a real impact on those of us sitting around this table. We all paid attention to what happened and kept up with the current events of the war. Nine years later, I joined the Marines partially due to what I learned and saw in the newsreels at the theater, and especially after I saw the movie *Guadalcanal Diary* in '43."

"Newsreels?" I asked. "What were those?"

"Back then," Lawson explained, "Newsreels were about the only way to see action films about the war or any other current events. Television didn't come into homes until later on. The radio and newspapers were available, but sometimes they were a little after the fact. We could read the news, but it was a day or longer before we got a hold of a paper with the latest. So, we turned on our radios or went to the movie theaters to see movies and to catch up on the news."

The men continued talking about their memories, but I pondered the statements of our former president, statements from a speech given under the gravest of circumstances. These men sitting around me felt the words were so important that they remembered every single one. My grandfather thought these powerful words and the actions taken by another country against our country were so significant that he remembered the words all these years.

Granddad had waited until he was eighteen to sign up for the Marines. He did not serve in World War Two, but he did serve in the Korean War. He would fight with the same commitment and love of country as soldiers before him. It was men like these, sitting around the table eating donuts in this small café, who made our country. These were the men I admired. I committed to living my life trying to be as brave as they had been.

If I made it off the operating table, I would try to live my life as they have lived theirs.

CHAPTER TEN

Painful Memories

I watched the hospital staff with great interest as they moved my body to another room. Relieved I had made it through the surgery, I wondered when I would be out of this floating state and back on the ground. I was still suspended in air. How much longer would I be in this state between solid matter and the afterlife?

From what I could tell, it looked like I was alive. The sheet wasn't pulled up covering my face, so I believed that was a good sign. My parents remained elsewhere, so I was in this new room alone except for the nurses who were in and out every few moments.

With a quick whoosh, time changed to another day with my grandfather. Once again, I saw myself getting into the car my grandfather kept as spotless and shiny as the day he bought it.

Even inside Granddad's car, my teeth chattered. "This is the coldest I have ever been." I noticed my voice sounded deeper than it did in the previous flashbacks to my earlier age of twelve.

"Not the coldest time for me," Granddad replied.

We sat in silence in the car as he turned toward the Donut Shop.

"What was it?" I asked.

"What?"

"What was the coldest day? The coldest temperature you've experienced?"

Granddad drove quietly down the road as if he hadn't heard my question.

Something clanked and took me back to the hospital. I heard more beeps. My body looked worse. Color had drained from my face on my lifeless body.

"Wait!" I said to myself. "I want to hear my grandfather's answer."

A deep, but soothing, Voice said, "Wes, you must return to your own body. It is not your time to join Me here. Your time is much later. You will make it through this. You will have another opportunity. When it is your time, you will join Me."

I remained high above my bed and looked down. My face turned a shade of gray. A sudden change in the beeping noises brought in an army of nurses and doctors and more equipment.

"Paddles!" someone screamed.

I watched, wondering what they were doing. The trunk of my body lifted off the table. My whole body jolted. *Please let me live*, I pleaded to God.

"Again!"

The beeping noises resumed at a slow and steady rate.

One doctor said, "Good. He is still with us."

Speaking to the Voice I had heard a few moments earlier, I silently said, *Thank you*. There was no answer but, in my mind, I knew God heard me. I knew He was with me at that moment. I felt His presence there.

A light flashed. The time changed, and I returned to the previous scene of years ago riding in the car with my grandfather. I heard my grandfather's answer.

"It was when I was in Korean."

"Sir?"

"When it was the coldest."

His remark caught me off guard because he had never spoken much about Korea. I'd been curious about the time he was in the war and had asked him when I was younger. But he always changed the subject. I did not know what he had experienced. And he never wanted to tell me, until now.

I looked at myself inside of Granddad's car. This version of me looked a couple of years older than before. I looked taller sitting in his car. Not yet old enough to drive, but perhaps I was now high school age, maybe fifteen. I was old enough at this point to know I should wait for Granddad's answer. But he wouldn't be rushed. The quietness continued as we left the car and entered the Donut Shop. Parker was seated with his plate full of donuts and coffee. He chewed and nodded to us.

"Good morning, Parker," Granddad said.

Jae handed us our own plates. "Be back with coffee."

Parker swallowed and said, "You two are awfully quiet this morning. Something wrong?"

"Not wrong. Wes here wanted to know about Korea."

Jae poured from a fresh pot of coffee and said, "Yes. Thank you, Marines." She went back to the counter and placed the coffee-pot back on the warmer before returning.

"Your grandfather, he saved my country, my family. All the Marines."

I looked to my grandfather for a response to Jae's comment.

Granddad shook his head. "Not me personally. She is talking about the great number of refugees saved during the war; some eventually brought here."

Jae nodded. "Yes, thank you, Marines."

"Now, Jae, we've told you many times, we were proud to do it. Good people in your country."

Jae returned to the counter, and Granddad turned to face Parker.

"Parker, Wes asked me about the coldest temperature I'd ever felt."

Parker shook his head as if he was shivering. "Oh. It makes me cold to think about it. Nearly lost toes because of the frostbite."

"Really?" I couldn't hide the surprise in my voice. "That was cold!"

Granddad continued, "It was. Trouble was, we walked and walked in the snow. The road had snow and icy patches. It was so cold. We walked a long way, probably several miles, and our feet were sweating. Then the sweat froze, and next came the frostbite."

"Your grandfather is telling the truth. I am not sure how

many of us lost toes, fingers, and even lives due to the cold. Frostbite is an ugly, gruesome thing. Turns the toes black, and of course, there are the blisters." Parker looked down at the table and added, "It was a tough walk. At the same time, we had to be aware of the enemy soldiers lurking along the way."

I chewed slowly. After I heard what both men had endured, and the description of frostbite, I almost lost my appetite. "Were a lot of people killed in Korea?"

Neither man responded at first. Then my grandfather said, "If you add everything together, all the soldiers on both sides and the people of the country, over a million people died. Yes, there was a lot of death."

Parker added, "At least your toes were thawed out when you walked out with a bullet in your behind to the hospital truck."

This was a story I'd never heard. "You had a bullet in your behind?"

Granddad's face turned a slight shade of red. "It wasn't a bullet. Only one piece of shrapnel. And it wasn't a hospital truck. It was just a jeep. But they took me to the tent hospital after I hobbled down on foot most of the way to the road."

"You walked? After you were hit?"

"Had to. It was the only way to get down off the hill. It was rocky and cold, and the ground was half-frozen. Couldn't get any transportation up there, no jeeps or trucks. Walking was the only way to get out of there."

A loud crashing noise startled me back to the position above my bed. I looked at my still body and then watched as my parents entered the room. Mom started crying, and Dad hugged her.

"He is going to be okay. The doctor said he will be okay. He is in a coma, but probably not for too long."

So that was it? Surgery was over. My heart had been shocked back to life. And now, I was in a coma?

Nurses came in and out but were not panicked.

A doctor entered the room. He examined my eyes with a bright light. I didn't see the light. I only saw him examining me as I watched from above.

"Yes, yes." The doctor's voice was raspy. "He seems to have stabilized now. Heart rate back to normal."

Mom attempted to talk between her sobs. "Is he..."

Dad interrupted, "I think she is asking if he is going to be all right. Will he come out of this?"

"Chances are good. He should be alert soon. We will monitor him and watch him closely. You two should go on home and get some rest. When he wakes up, the nurses will call you right away."

They nodded and slowly left the room.

My grandfather's voice transported me back to the Donut Shop. He continued his story about being in Korea and how cold it was walking back to the road.

"I had to walk down off the hill for over a mile to the road. We were dug in up at the top and somehow a bullet found me. My buddies lifted me up out of that hole and helped me stand on my feet. Once I got moving around, I made it to the road. Wasn't sure exactly where I was going, but I kept walking, and I was lucky no one fired at me. Once I walked for a while, I saw the hospital tent down the way, and I just kept moving. Then a jeep came by when I was nearly at the hospital tent and gave me a ride the rest of the way.

"I could hear the firing and explosions up on the hill and I worried about my buddies. Most of them made it through that skirmish. But there was another battle...well, I'll save that story for another time. It wears me out to talk about that one."

Parker, typically silent, decided to say a few words about the Korean War. "Wes, your grandfather is hesitant to tell you about the other battle on the ridge because so many of his buddies died in that one. He was lucky to have survived it himself."

Granddad didn't say anything more. He quietly finished his donuts and coffee. For a moment, the table was silent.

Lawson, who'd joined us sometime during my absence, used my grandfather's silence as an opportunity to start a new conversation. "Did you hear about the dinner at the VFW hall tonight?"

"What's a VFW?" I asked.

"It means Veterans of Foreign Wars," Lawson explained.

Jimmy had a smirk on his face. "Are you going? To the VFW? And, more importantly, you taking Maribel?"

"Yes, I am going, and Maribel is going with me," he said and grinned.

"You'd better be ready to hear the gossip next week." Jimmy laughed.

CHAPTER ELEVEN

Purpose

Back in the hospital, my mom was excited. She'd noticed my fingers moving. Only thing was, I wasn't trying to move them.

I didn't feel my fingers or the sheet underneath my fingers moving back and forth. My mom was smiling and talking cheerfully to my dad. I wasn't quite sure of the significance because I was still above looking down at me rather than looking up at my parents from my bed. I had no feeling of moving my fingers on the sheet. Perhaps the movement was some kind of reflex? Or random nerve firing?

A nurse came into the room. "Well now, Wes, it looks like you'll be joining us soon."

Mom said, "I knew it. I knew he would be okay. I've been praying all day."

The nurse looked my mother in the eye and said, "Mrs. Williams, remember what the doctor said. It could be a long recovery. It will take a while to see exactly how Wes will function. We must see if the time his brain was without oxygen had any lasting effects."

Long recovery? I was eager to get back to my own life. I missed home, and I wanted to return to school.

Mom nodded. "I understand. We will pray for his recovery and strength."

The nurse nodded and looked at the monitors.

I dozed once again. It was a dark and murky-looking space. Then I was caught up above my own body and transported back to the earlier time. I had wanted to have at least one last visit to the past before I came completely back to earth, and it looked like my wish was granted.

It was delightful seeing Granddad once again opening the door to the Donut Shop and standing straight up as he walked inside at a regular pace. Being at the shop with the men felt like home. It was comfortable here. I had no worries or stress. The prior week of school was forgotten. Eager to listen to the newest stories and jokes of the group, I followed Granddad inside. Here, I had my grandfather's undivided attention. I felt respected and valued by all, even though I was a teenager.

Granddad and I were the last of the bunch to enter the shop.

"You two sleep in?" Lawson asked.

"Nah," Granddad said, "had to go by the Post Office first thing this morning."

"Lawson's asking because he is excited to tell you all about his date with Maribel." Jimmy chuckled.

Granddad laughed. "I want to hear every detail."

We retrieved our plates piled with donuts that Jae had already prepared and left on the countertop for us. She followed us to the table with the coffeepot and cups.

"Well, let me guess. Maribel stood you up?" Granddad joked.

"Not even close. We had a grand time, thank you. And we set another date."

Listening to these men talk about who was dating who, seeing who, and the general gossip of the day reminded me of my own high school friends.

"Lawson, you would think you'd have better things to do than occupy your mind with women all the time," Old Walt said.

"I have plenty to do and think about," Lawson replied. "I've always had a purpose in life."

"Oh, your main purpose must be trying to date every woman in town who will talk to you." Old Walt slapped Lawson on the back and laughed.

"Nope, but at least they do talk to me."

"Well then, Lawson," my grandfather pressed, "if your purpose isn't women, tell us your purpose for life."

"Oh," Jimmy chimed in, "These days he's lucky to get out of bed without creaking and popping every one of his joints, much less have a purpose."

"Now wait just a minute," Old Walt said. "You are hitting a little too close to home. When I get out of bed in the mornings, the way my joints pop and crack, it sounds like an entire drum section of the Fort Worth Symphony Orchestra."

"Still waiting," Granddad said.

"For what?" Lawson asked.

"To hear your purpose in life."

"Oh, his purpose now is to get something on sale down at the hardware store." Parker laughed.

"Did you hear that?" Lawson asked. "Parker cracked a joke!"

Parker laughed along with everyone else. We all knew that Parker rarely made jokes.

Granddad continued eating his donut and listening to the conversation. I knew he was expecting Lawson to make a comment about his main goal for the day. After a bit, Granddad could wait no longer. "Okay, Lawson, do you have any plans for the day or a purpose in mind?"

"Nope."

"See, like I said, no purpose." Granddad laughed.

Then my grandfather turned to me with a serious look on his face. He didn't make this expression very often, so I knew I needed to pay close attention.

"And you, young Wes, what is your purpose? Had any thoughts about that?"

"No sir. Not much. I know I want to go to college."

"Studying a lot? Making good grades and all that?" Granddad asked.

"Yes, sir."

"Good to hear."

The rest of the visit that morning was another round of jokes between the group. But my grandfather's question about my own purpose for my life made me curious. I had no idea what I wanted to do or what my purpose was for my future. I didn't want to ask him in front of the others, but truth was, I had no clue what I wanted to do for the rest of my life. I waited until the ride back home to bring it up again.

As soon as we left the Donut Shop and got into the car, I asked, "Granddad, is it wrong that I am not sure what I want to do in life? I mean, I am almost sixteen."

"Not at all. The only thing I knew I wanted to do at your age was join the Marines. And if World War Two hadn't happened when I was a boy, I wouldn't have wanted to join the military. But that war, well, it changed things in the country."

"When did you realize you wanted to be a draftsman with the power company?"

"Oh, that came about later. It was kind of a job of opportunity. I had taken a couple of courses. But the actual job wasn't something I knew about at your age."

"So, I shouldn't worry if I don't know yet? What I want to do?"

"No, son. It is more important to have a good, strong faith in God and live your life as you know He wants you to. Even I didn't know about the important things until I was in the Korean War."

"Oh?"

Granddad was silent. To me, the silence was uneasy. I knew Granddad wanted to say more but was hesitant at the same time.

"Wes, you remember not long ago when Parker mentioned a battle that happened on the ridge. In Korea?"

"Yes sir."

"What say you and I go to my house for a bit? I'll make us another pot of coffee. We can sit out on the front porch, and I'll tell you all about it."

"Yes sir. I would like that."

My heart rate increased as I anticipated this story. This was the story I'd wondered about for years. From time to time, I heard others mention the battle on the ridge. Even when my grandmother was living, she would caution me not to bring up the battle on the ridge. And now, I would at last hear Granddad talk about it.

A shift in time found me back at the hospital.

Wait! I must hear Granddad's story. I had been too young to appreciate it the one time I'd heard it before. *But I want to hear it again.*

I saw my mother combing my hair. I was sleeping. Or rather, I remained in a coma. Why had I been yanked out of the past where I could hear my grandfather? I wanted to return there and listen to him.

The Voice was back. I knew it was not my grandfather. It was God speaking again. I knew it by the tone of Voice and the peacefulness that overtook my mind.

"Wes, this is your last story. You will soon join your parents again. You are going to be back on earth. After today, you will no longer be here in the past. When you emerge, you will be different."

"But, sir, how?" I whispered to the voice I knew had to be God. "Sir?"

Silence.

Wait! Please, I want to hear my grandfather's story once more.

Ready to hear the story from my grandfather, I waited. I was in-between. Nothing I could do but wait to be taken back to the earlier years.

CHAPTER TWELVE

The Ridge

I looked down at my hospital room and saw the familiar scene: the white sheet and single blanket across my still body, machines beeping, and the constant visits by nurses checking on this thing or that. I noticed my hands moving from time to time. And I moved my leg once. For the most part, I remained in the world between earth and heaven. I'd been in this state for what seemed like months. Truth was, I had no way of knowing exactly how long I had been here or when I would return to earth for good. The Voice had told me I would hear only one more story of the past, but I had no idea when that would happen or how long I had been in this current state. Had I been in the hospital for days, weeks, or months? I wondered how long my recovery would be and when I might get back to my regular life. But for right now, I wanted to hear the rest of Granddad's story.

A quick zoom through time and I was back in the car with my grandfather. He turned the car into his semi-circular driveway and pulled it around to the front door. Placing the car in park, he said, "I'll get the coffee going. I think it is warm enough in the sun to sit on the porch."

"Sounds good to me. Need help with the coffee?"

"No, I've got it, but thank you."

I sat in one of the two wooden rockers on the porch. The flags flew high on the pole, the American flag on top and the Marine Corp flag beneath Old Glory.

"Here you are," Granddad said, handing me my cup.

I sipped and waited for him to begin. I had asked him about

the war in Korea before and I knew this story would be difficult for him to tell.

"Wes, you know when we talked about the frostbite and how we slowly made our way down to the road?"

"Yes sir."

"That happened long after the ridge. In fact, I had regrouped with another bunch after the battle on the ridge."

I sat silently, anticipating what he would say next.

Granddad rocked in his chair and sipped his coffee. "You see, one day it seemed quiet. We had settled down into our foxholes. We hadn't heard so much as a peep from the enemy. We knew the days ahead would be fierce. We were trying to take back the ridge a little bit at a time. The enemy was determined to keep that ridge, and the Marines were determined to move past it into the territory of the North Koreans. It was probably near midnight before I dozed off. I remember listening for any crack of a branch, a twig, anything that sounded like footsteps, or even someone breathing heavily or clearing their throat. It was completely silent. And completely dark. Made it hard to see if anyone was sneaking up on our group. It was hard to relax in that situation. If we hadn't been so exhausted, none of us would have slept until we returned home… for those of us blessed enough to make it back."

More silence.

I patiently waited for Granddad to continue and watched as small birds landed on a Live Oak tree in the front yard near the porch. The sun warmed my face.

"Our First Marine Division made its way up there near what was known as the Punchbowl and Kan Mu Bong Ridge. At that point, we had actually crossed the boundary and were in North Korea."

"Really? You were across enemy lines?"

"At the time, the North Koreans held that territory, that ridge. We were, as they say, behind enemy lines in some places. That little stretch of land was as important to them as it was to us. We needed to gain that ground. It would prove we were advancing against an enemy who outnumbered us.

"The Marines had been gathering up around the area for days, planning at last to take the hill. Our military superiors organized the assault. My company, Fox Company, was among the Marines sent in to take the hill. From our vantage point, we could see the Navy's gunfire at night because we were near the east coast of Korea. From where we were, we even felt the ground shaking from the gunfire of the ships off the coast. It seemed sudden and out of nowhere that we were hit quickly by the loudest, nonstop storm of artillery fire we had heard since arriving in Korea. It continued for hours. We were outnumbered and couldn't determine the location of their military. The assault didn't cease. They kept coming at us and coming at us. When their men were close enough, they used bayonets to finish off many of our men. We hailed the enemy with grenades. They had been hiding in their bunkers. They came running out. Some of our guys went inside the tunnels and bunkers using bayonets."

My grandfather was silent for a few moments. I thought he must have been living the battle in his mind all over again.

"We advanced up the ridge. Some of the Marines crawled on the ground. Others were on their knees or walking stooped down, trying to hide. All of us trying to dodge bullets. The enemy ran into the tunnels between bunkers. They'd hide and then emerge out of nowhere. The nights were the toughest. The battle lasted for days."

I sensed his anxiety as he relayed the story to me. But he continued.

"Sometimes at night...the screams of the men," he paused again. "The sounds of war can haunt you the rest of your life. There was nothing I could do but continue fighting. I felt the wet dirt on my knees, smelled the stink of gunfire, and heard the cries of dying men. It didn't seem like it could be real. It was too horrible to be real. But it was.

"After nonstop fighting, day and night, the grenades and bullets finally began to take a toll on the enemy. The battle continued back and forth. At times, advancing. And sometimes, the enemy pushed us back. We weren't certain if we were making much headway. Every inch of ground was precious. Once we gained a little distance and made progress across the line. We fought as hard as possible to keep them from trying to take it back.

"The fighting continued the whole next day. They pushed us. We moved forward again. It was almost sunrise before the bullets and hail fire of artillery quieted. It wasn't until daybreak…"

I didn't look directly at my grandfather. I knew he was crying. He pretended he wasn't. He rocked back and forth in his chair and sipped his coffee. I knew he was remembering his buddies who did not make it home.

After a couple of minutes, he spoke. "Wes, when the firing stopped…"

I waited.

"Only twelve of us walked out alive."

Out of the corner of my eye, I watched Granddad bury his face in his hands. I refrained from speaking.

Finally, Granddad spoke again. "It was the moment I walked out of there—that was when I knew what my life would be about. I decided right then if I made it all the way back here to Texas alive, I would be someone the others, the ones who died, would be proud of. They couldn't come back home. I would do what I could for their families and friends. I would support the Marines and this country. But most importantly, I would have a stronger faith in God and live like He wanted me to.

"Now, Wes, I know you haven't been in a war. I pray you will never have to see those things and feel that fear. But the one thing I would pray for is that you would experience a strong faith in God."

"Yes sir."

"That would be the most important thing to me and your parents. We want to know you are a good person. You think about others. You care. You try to help when people need it. You love God and our country. Other than that, it doesn't matter how you decide to make a living. That will come. You will find something to study or an occupation you like. You will find someone special, marry, and have a family. But those things don't matter if you aren't a good person. Nothing matters if you don't believe in God."

"Yes sir."

I knew this was the last time I would visit my younger self and the last time Granddad would tell me that same story. I knew I would soon return to the present day.

Something felt different. I no longer had the feeling of being buoyant in the air. I was stable. I was back on earth. I wasn't above my bed; I was in it. I was inside my own body once again. Now I felt the pain in my leg. My head throbbed. Maybe the escape back in time helped me not feel this pain. But now, I felt it. I felt it all over my body. What would happen now? How would my life change? Would I be able to get out of this bed and back to living?

CHAPTER THIRTEEN

Same Body, Different State of Mind

There was no way to explain to people what my mind had been through. Would this be described as an "out-of-body" experience or "life after death" or "near death"? I thought about this for some time. After all, I had been in this world and back out again into the air. What is that called? Partial afterlife? Almost dead?

And I heard *His* voice. Is that considered having a vision? A dream? A visit? I had no clue. Would other people think I was just hearing voices? Hallucinating? Experiencing delusions? No, He was with me, and I was with Him. I knew that. I had no doubt.

One thing I knew for certain—my life would be different, just as He said. I had been given a second chance. I had a "do-over." I could live life more fully, with more meaning. I would take nothing for granted. Ever.

I opened my eyes slightly. Everything was blurry. In fact, nothing was distinguishable other than light and shadows. But the pain continued. I hoped someone would give me more medicine to stop this pain.

I heard mumbling. People talking. But I could not distinguish the words. Low tones, almost whispering. I strained to hear better and concentrated as hard as I could.

"Look at his eyes," my mom declared.

A shadowy figure approached my bedside. "Wes? Son, are you awake?"

Mom called the nurse on the intercom. "Can you come in here?"

A nurse soon joined my parents.

"Well, Wes," the nurse said, "It looks like you are coming around. Let me look at everything here."

A bright light, right into my pupils.

That's awful. Please stop the torture. I wanted to say those words to the nurse, but I could not speak. My mouth refused to move, and no sounds came out. *God, Help me speak soon. Help me remember how to work my mouth and how to speak. Thank you for being with me here in the hospital and for always staying with me. Amen.*

"Yes, Mr. and Mrs. Williams, he looks like he is coming around. Let's not excite him. Just stay with him. He still needs a great deal of rest. If he wakes up, offer him some water. His throat is probably still dry and sore from the tube we removed yesterday."

Tube?

Mom took my hand as I had seen her do often during my stay in the hospital. This time was different. I felt her hand. The warmth and comfort from her touch felt wonderful. I had missed this sensation while I was in between the spaces of earth and heaven.

It wasn't long before a doctor came in to check on me. "I heard the good news. Wes was trying to open his eyes?"

"Yes, he was!" I heard the excitement in Mom's voice. "He moved his fingers a bit more today."

"That's wonderful. Let's have a look."

This time, I felt the doctor as he uncovered my legs and exposed my feet, one at a time. I noticed the cast on my leg. *What happened to my leg? How did it get injured? How am I supposed to get around with that clunky cast on my leg?*

The doctor ran a cold, hard object along the bottom of my foot on the leg without the cast. I could feel the metal, like it was his ballpoint pen or something. It was strange.

Whoa! That tickles!

"This is good news. See how his foot reacted this time? Instead of the simple reflex we have seen in the past weeks, he moved his whole leg up, like it tickled him. Good to see him reacting. He felt the sensation rather than just a simple nerve reflex. His brain swelling is continuing to go down. He is getting more feeling back in his feet and legs."

Again, the bright light in my eyes.

Why do you people keep doing that? And why can't I talk to you?

"Okay," the doctor continued. "Let me check all his connections. Good...That's good...Everything looks great. Now, Wes, can you open your eyes?"

I'm trying.

I struggled and managed to open my eyes just a bit. My vision still wasn't good. My eyes closed again even though I wanted to keep them open.

"All signs are improving," the doctor reported. "We hope he will come around more in the coming days."

"Oh!" my mother exclaimed, "That is wonderful news!"

"Now, Mr. and Mrs. Williams, understand that his improvements may take some time," the doctor said, "but we are seeing some good signs here today. Remember, he was without oxygen for some time after the wreck, and we aren't sure how long. He also was without oxygen after the surgery when his heart stopped. There may be some injury to the brain. It might be slight or none at all. We will take each day as it comes."

A wreck? I was in a wreck? I don't even remember driving. What happened? And a brain injury? Please, God, no.

"We will continue to pray, Doctor," Mom said.

"Good. Prayer never hurt anyone. I will check back tomorrow. This is a good day. A good day indeed. And Nurse Abby, you call me if anything happens."

"Yes, Doctor."

I dozed off, but this time, I remained here on earth. There were no visits back in time. I knew I would never see Jimmy again since he'd passed away. And I knew the next time I saw my grandfather he would be limping along with his walker. But somehow, the joy of seeing them as they once were, seeing Jimmy one last time, still felt warm in my heart. I would hold those memories forever.

A nurse yanked the curtain open, and a bright light flashed

right on my face. "Good morning, Mr. Wes! I heard you had a big day yesterday! Now, let's check you out."

Once again, the poking, prodding, and shining the bright light into my eyes started. *How does anyone get well with all this torture?*

"I reckon your parents will be in pretty soon. Let's get you cleaned up a bit first."

Whoa, this is embarrassing! She quickly sponged me over and dried every inch of me. I could have done without the spectacle. The strange thing was it felt good to be cleaned up. I wondered how many of these sponge baths I'd had since I had been here and never felt a single one until today. I figured being aware of the bathing routine was probably a good sign.

"Juan will come in later and give you a quick shave."

Shave? Someone has been shaving my face? I'd never noticed.

Next, the nurse changed the sheets. I suppose this routine had been repeated each day too.

I heard the door opening.

"Good morning, Wes," my mom said.

"I just cleaned him up for your visit. Juan will shave him when he comes by. Your son's vital signs are looking good. He may wake up more today. But don't be alarmed if he doesn't or if you are not here when he wakes. He is not aware of the time of day and may wake up in the night."

"Thank you," my mother said.

Mom took my hand, and I felt her sit down on the side of my bed. "Your father will be here in a few minutes. He went to pick up Granddad."

This got my attention. I wanted to see Granddad. I knew that to talk to him I needed to open my eyes. I wanted to see him. I wanted to tell him about how much he meant to me. I wanted him to know that all the stories I'd heard at the Donut Shop were important to me.

I tried to open my eyes, but I suddenly felt very tired. Sleep overtook me once again. It was out of my control. I couldn't fight it. I dozed off into a deep sleep.

Voices interrupted my peaceful nap. I mustered up as much strength as I could. I wanted to hear them. What were they saying? One voice sounded like it could be Granddad's voice.

"Just tell him I will come another time."

Wait! I want to see you!

I attempted to move my arm. I wanted to wave at them and get their attention. I didn't want my grandfather to leave.

I attempted to say "wait" but "wa–" was the only thing sound that came out. *Why won't my mouth do what I want it to? I am thinking the right word! It just won't come out!*

"Oh! He said something!" my mom said.

"What? What, Wes?" my dad asked.

With all my effort, I whispered "Granddad", but it came out more like a soft-spoken "Gra–da." That must have been close enough, because my mom reacted. She broke out in what people call an ugly cry. Full-blown boo-hooing and sniffling. She grabbed a handful of tissues out of the box on the night table.

Dad was ecstatic. "Wes! You spoke!"

My grandfather used his walker and slowly made his way to my bedside. "Wes, welcome back." He held on to the walker to steady himself with one hand and took my hand with his other hand. "Wes, my boy."

Grandad's hand was reassuring. I knew it was him in the present time. I was elated he was here. There was so much I wanted to say to him. I wanted to hug him. As much as I wanted to reach out to him, I couldn't. At least I could see him and sense his hand on mine. I tried to keep my eyes on him, wanting to say words I couldn't yet speak.

I knew I was in a different state of mind and not in the past. I was in the present time. I could think about the future. I would leave this hospital and be like I was before the wreck. Someday soon, I would tell them everything, but for today, I would concentrate on feeling better and getting stronger. When the time was right, I'd tell Granddad the details. I'd let him know I *did* hear his words from years ago when he told me about the most important things in life. Not only would I tell him that, but I'd show him

I planned to live my life as he had his. I would make it a point to prove to him, and my parents, that my life would count for good. I would have strong faith, just like Granddad and my parents wanted me to have.

CHAPTER FOURTEEN

Clean, Confused, and Dazed

After all the excitement of being able to utter partial words and open my eyes, exhaustion became my constant companion. Unable to travel back in time again, I tried my hardest to re-play each episode in my mind. I envisioned the Donut Shop. I attempted to bring the stories back, but I couldn't. I remembered talking with Jimmy as if he were still alive. I remembered seeing my grandfather walking straight, upright, and strong, just like he did a few years ago. I remembered the stories about Lawson fighting a gorilla and Parker's father finding papers on the ship. I remembered Old Walt's ranch stories and the cattle in the lightning storm. I thought about Old Walt's ranch, his leathery, sun-worn face, and the time he was in the Marines.

"Good morning, Wes. Ready for your sponge bath?"

Not again. So embarrassing.

The nurse went through the same routine as last time. Another nurse came in and out as this nurse bathed me. They chatted with each other, but I wasn't able to make out the words.

Then the first nurse did something strange. Maybe she had done this every day before and I slept through it. She rolled me from side to side and talked the whole time.

"Now, we are going to change your sheets."

Another nurse came in and assisted with this ordeal. I was moved back and forth. They lifted my feet. They placed new pillows under my head.

No wonder I am so tired. These people don't let me rest.

"Now, there you go, Wes. All cleaned up," the first nurse said. She gathered up the linens and went to the door.

"Phil will shave you today. He will be in before your parents get here."

I slept once again. I suspected it may have been only a few moments before the sound of someone entering the room woke me up. It was Phil.

"Hey, bud. Let's get you shaved. Should just take a minute."

The buzz of the electric shaver tickled my face. I supposed it was another sign of me being more alert.

Phil left at the same time my parents arrived.

"He looks about the same as yesterday," my father observed.

"Sleeping like a baby," Mom noted.

But I heard you. I thought I was awake. Am I?

"You stay here with him," Dad said. "My dad called, and his car is in the shop. I'll go pick him up. But first, he said he wanted to run by the Donut Shop and say hi to his buddies and grab a donut. Might be a few minutes." Dad kissed Mom and left.

Granddad's return visit was good news. I wanted to talk to Granddad. In fact, I wanted to talk to everyone. I wanted to know what happened to me. How long was I in a coma? What happened in the wreck? Was I with anyone? Why did I need surgery, twice? I had a lot of questions. If only I could move my mouth today. I had to remember how to do it. I used to take talking for granted. Now, I appreciated each syllable.

Mom combed my hair again. "Carol Ann has been asking to come see you. I told her it might be better to wait."

Carol Ann? Who was that? Was that my girlfriend? A neighbor? A cousin? I couldn't remember anything about her. If I don't remember her, it was best not to have her come visit, whoever she was.

Mom was quiet. She didn't say anything else until the nurse came back in. "How did he sleep last night? Restful?"

"Yes, he did. The doctor came back by around midnight and checked him over."

He did? I slept through that? I hadn't noticed the doctor at all.

Sleeping was all I did.

Mom must have turned on the television in the room because I heard an announcer. It sounded like a game, or maybe the news. Some sounds and voices confused me.

The door opened again.

"How's my boy?" Granddad asked.

I wanted to answer him. I tried again to open my eyes. I was determined to open them while Granddad was here.

Then, I did it. I opened my eyes! The light from the window blinded me, and I instantly closed my eyes. I tried to open them once more, but slowly this time.

"Ah, there he is," Dad said. "Wes?"

I couldn't answer him, but I did hold my eyes open for a bit. It seemed like a long time but might have been seconds. And then they shut again. I slept. I thought I was sleeping heavily, but I heard voices talking. It sounded like several voices. One I identified as my grandfather.

"Gra–da," I muttered.

My mother, father, and grandfather huddled around my bed.

"Listen, did you hear that?" Mom asked. "I think he said Granddad."

"I'm here, my boy." Granddad scooted closer to the bed with his walker. He grabbed my hand.

I did it! They understood me!

I opened my eyes. Granddad was there. I attempted a smile, but I'm not sure it was detected. "Do...nu," I muttered.

"What did he say? Do now? Do new? Don't?" Dad asked.

I opened my eyes as much as possible. It felt like they were wide open, but I had no way of knowing. I wanted to tell Granddad: *No! Donut! Donut Shop!*

"Do–nu," I muttered.

Mom smiled. "I think he wants us to go get him some donuts!"

Then, with all my might, I shook my head as much as possible to say "no."

"No," Grandad said. "I don't think that's it."

"Are you hungry?" my dad asked.

This was frustrating. My mouth wouldn't work along with the words my brain was thinking. I wasn't communicating what I wanted to say. My parents and grandfather tried to figure out what I was saying, and our back-and-forth lasted a while. After that, I was exhausted. I fell asleep with Granddad still holding my hand. I don't know how long he was there. I slept the rest of the day and didn't wake until the next day.

That morning, when the door opened, I heard a new voice. It was a man. He asked the nurse where my parents were and said he needed to speak with Mr. and Mrs. Williams.

"They should be in soon," the nurse replied.

"I'll check back later. Can you give them my card? They can call me if they like," the man said.

"Police Sergeant Clark?"

"Yes ma'am."

"I will let them know."

Why would a policeman want my parents to call?

I dozed off and on for a few minutes. I wondered if the medicine they gave me made me more tired. I didn't like the feeling. I wanted to be awake and talk to people. It was a struggle.

"Good morning, Wes." My mom's voice broke through my sleep.

I opened my eyes a bit.

"There you are," she said. "Your father is parking the car."

The nurse entered my room. "Mrs. Williams, a policeman left this for you. He said to call if you like."

"Thank you. This must be about the police report of the wreck."

What happened in the wreck? Somebody tell me.

The nurse left.

Mom held my hand and said, "Wes, I am thankful each day you are with us. We were very blessed when you were born."

My father joined us in the room.

"This man left his card," my mother told him.

"I'll step outside and give him a call."

Mom combed my hair and talked to me softly. "Your grandfather is coming by later today. And soon, we'll find out from the police what happened in the wreck. It's been a few weeks. But we'll find out soon."

A few weeks? I have been in this hospital for a few weeks? It felt like years.

Dad came back into the room. "Sergeant Clark is on his way. He will bring the report with him."

The room was quiet. I sensed my parents were anxious about this report. I prayed I had done nothing wrong. In all honesty, I had no idea what had happened.

Hearing the door open, I managed to open my eyes again. A man entered the room.

"Sergeant Clark?" my dad asked, extending his hand.

"Yes, Mr. and Mrs. Williams? Nice to meet you. I brought the report by for you. I knew you would likely be at the hospital and might not be able to come by the station to pick it up. But I thought you would want to read it for yourself. Do you have an attorney? Someone you can call to help you with this? You'll want an attorney who specializes in auto accidents. I imagine you will need some assistance."

"Thank you. Let us look this over and talk about it," Dad said.

"Of course. You have my number if you need anything."

"Thank you," my mother said.

"Well, hon, let's have a look."

Tell me, tell me, I silently pleaded to them. Perhaps they didn't realize I could hear people when my eyes were shut.

My mother skimmed the report. "Oh my goodness!"

"Yes," Dad said. "I agree with Sergeant Clark. Looks like we might need the help of an attorney."

I pried my eyes open. There was no other way to describe it. I mentally envisioned myself prying them open. It was a massive effort to raise my eyelids. I wanted to communicate to my parents that I needed to know what had happened.

I watched my parents read the report again from the beginning to the end.

Tell me. Read it to me, I silently begged. *What happened in the wreck?*

CHAPTER FIFTEEN

Real Food?

The days followed one after another. Most of my tubes had been disconnected by now, and. I had more moments of being awake and opening my eyes. I heard conversations, but the one thing I had not heard was what happened the day of the wreck. I waited for someone to say something, anything that would give me a hint. Was the wreck my fault? I assumed it was because my parents had contacted an attorney. I knew this because I heard them mention the attorney's name: Keller.

And so I waited. I waited to eat real food. I waited to move on my own and to use my leg with the cast on it. I waited to hear about the wreck. I waited to eat on my own and dress myself. I waited and struggled to speak the words I thought in my mind. Waiting was difficult.

Then, one day, things changed. I had been awake for a while and felt stronger. I felt a slight sense of promise and strength. And I felt even more promise when I heard my grandfather say, "Wes, I brought you a donut. And some black coffee. Now, don't you tell that nurse, you know, the bossy one who gives orders like a Marine."

For some reason, Granddad's comment made me want to laugh. I couldn't help it. It was just like something Granddad would have said to Jimmy or one of his other buddies at the Donut Shop.

A tiny chuckle came out.

"Are you laughing?" Granddad asked.

I opened my eyes and looked right at him. I even attempted a nod. Maybe a tiny nod happened. I don't know. But I grinned at him, and he smiled right back.

"Now, that's my boy."

The nurse opened the door and noticed the donuts and coffee on my table.

"Mr. Williams, I hope you weren't planning on letting Wes eat that."

"Oh no, no," he said. He tried as hard as he could not to smile.

A smile emerged all the way across my face after I heard Granddad's denial, and I was afraid I had given away his attempt to smuggle in donuts for me.

"Well, will you look at that?" the nurse said. "He's smiling."

I turned my head and looked at Granddad again, who was waiting patiently for the nurse to leave. It was incredible to see him. I wanted to tell him about my near-death experience. I wanted to recount the stories I had heard for a second time and let him know that this time, at seventeen, I better understood what the stories and jokes were all about.

I smiled again at the thought of Granddad defying the doctor's orders. It was just like him, a hardheaded Marine with a giant heart.

"Today," the nurse said as she checked my vitals, "we'll try to get you to sit up a bit, drink through a straw, and eat a bite or two of food. Soft food." She turned and gave Granddad a stern look. "Then you'll be able to get this last IV out of your arm. And after that, we will try solid foods. And maybe way after that, you can give him a donut."

Now Granddad laughed. He and I both knew he was busted.

Today was another day in the hospital, but this one would be better. I just had that feeling. This was the day I would be given food. Well, at least soft food, as the nurse said.

A few minutes later, an assistant barged through the door carrying a plastic tray with what looked like a plastic flying saucer on it.

"Here we go, Wes," the assistant said. He slapped the tray onto my table and scooped the flying saucer up to reveal a small bowl and glass of juice underneath.

What IS that stuff? I thought the nurse said food. Not baby food. Well, whatever the goop is, I want to try and keep it down.

The nurse waited for the assistant to leave before dipping a spoon into the bowl. "Now, Wes, let's see if you want this."

I opened my mouth, and the nurse touched the spoon to my tongue. "There, just a little apple sauce. What do you think?"

It felt funny in my mouth, but I gave it a go. *One step at a time.*

"Now, swallow that on down," she said and wiped my mouth.

Is this it? I'm going to be fed like a baby? I have to get better than this!

"Okay, well, that's a start. Let's try another spoonful."

She fed me a few more after that.

"Now, let's be sure you can keep this down. We'll go slow. We can try again in a little while, and then later today, we'll take this last tube out of your arm."

She wiped my mouth once more. "Okay, let's get your face cleaned up."

Here we go again.

"Your PT will be right in. We're going to get you moving a little today."

I smiled.

"Yes, I thought you would like that."

My grandfather sat in a chair by the bed, his walker folded up beside the chair. "Now, my dear Wes, I am going to help you learn how to sit and walk again. I had to learn it, too. After my surgeries that went haywire."

I smiled at him. I muttered what I hoped was "thank you," but I'm not sure it came out that way.

"That's okay, son. You'll get your speech back, too. We'll take it slow." Granddad looked at me a moment and, as if a light had gone off, he said, "You know, if talking is hard, maybe we can get you to write things down until you have your speech back."

I managed a small nod of my head.

"Hey there, Wes," a man not much older than me said as he opened the door. "I'm Alexander, but you can call me Alex. I'm your physical therapist."

I nodded.

"Nice to meet you, too. Today, I'm just gonna have a look and see where we are. Then we can work out a plan to get you going."

"Alex," Granddad said, "I would like to help, you know, encourage him. So, can you tell me what the plan will be once you have it worked up?"

Alex looked at my grandfather's walker and hesitated.

I smiled and nodded again to show Alex my approval.

"Of course. If Wes wants you to help, that would be a great help to me as well."

Alex lifted my limbs, one at a time. He asked me to try and move this way or that. He gave me commands, but I failed most of them. It was a struggle. I'd tell my arm to raise or my leg to move, but they'd only move a tiny bit. I tried as hard as possible, too. I reached down deep to retrieve every ounce of strength I had, but nothing seemed to work like I wanted.

At the end of the evaluation, Alex said, "Wes, you're not in such bad shape. Part of the reason you're having difficulty is because you have been in a coma for..." He glanced at my chart. "Almost two months. This means your muscles lost their strength. But we'll build you back up. I could tell you tried to and wanted to move as I asked, but for the most part, the movements were very slight. And, of course, you'll have to gradually put more weight on that leg with the protective cast. The best news is your brain is sending the commands to your muscles. In other words, we're at a good starting place. We'll keep an eye on your weaker leg and make sure it returns to normal. It might take a bit longer, but we'll get started on it soon."

I felt a smile cover my entire face. I wanted to say "thank you" but muttered something else entirely. I suppose I sounded very confused. I understood what Alex said, but he couldn't understand me.

"Sounds like we are on a roll," Granddad said.

I smiled again.

My parents entered the room.

"Sorry, we are running a little late, but we went by to see the attorney about the accident," Dad said.

"I explained our therapy plan to Wes and his grandfather. Here is the evaluation report. I can get you another copy if you need it for your attorney," Alex said.

What are they talking about? Please, someone tell me about the accident.

My father looked over the report. "Thank you. We might need an extra copy."

Alex propped me up in the hospital bed. "Need any more blankets?"

I shook my head "no."

"I will see you tomorrow, and we'll get started with some exercises to strengthen those muscles of yours."

"What time, Alex?" Granddad asked.

"It will be after ten, probably ten-thirty or so."

"Thank you, Alex."

My dad asked, "Are you going to help Alex with the therapy like we talked about?"

"Yes. I think it will be helpful. Now, what did the attorney say?" Granddad asked.

Yes! What did the attorney say? What happened in the wreck?

CHAPTER SIXTEEN

A Simple Message

I waited for someone to answer Granddad's question. I prayed at last to know how I ended up here, in a hospital bed, unable to speak or move much.

Granddad cleared his throat and asked again, "How did it go with the attorney?"

"We thought it went well," my dad replied. "Mr. Keller thinks we have a case. But, since Wes is almost eighteen and he would be eighteen before we go to court, we need to see what he thinks when he is able to tell us. He will have to agree to what Mr. Keller is proposing."

"I see. Have you told Wes?" Granddad asked.

"No, we didn't think he could understand everything going on," Mom replied. "And, he has been sleeping most of the time since his last surgery."

I could take it no longer. I had to know. I needed to communicate with my parents that I wanted to know. The anxiety was too much to bear. I concentrated on the words. I attempted to make my mouth say them. *Tell me*, I thought. *Please tell me what happened.*

"T...t..." My mouth moved slightly to say the word "tell," but the "t" sound was the only noise that came out.

"Wes, would you like to know?" Mom asked.

I managed a slight nod.

"You were in a wreck. You were driving home from school late in the afternoon near dusk on the farm road that curves right after the stop sign. You know, where you take the fork in the road toward our neighborhood?"

I looked at Mom, hoping she knew I was listening.

"You understand?"

I nodded again.

My dad took over the storytelling. "Another car approached from the other direction. Right where you are supposed to take the fork in the road, the car cut in front of you and hit you head-on. Your car rolled over in the ditch. It took hours to get you out. The doctors weren't certain of how badly your head was injured at that time. Once in the hospital, it took two surgeries to put you back together. You had to have a metal rod put in your right leg, and then you had internal bleeding in your abdomen. The scans of your head looked pretty good, well, except for the swelling. The swelling is causing you to have difficulty with your speech. At least that is what the doctor thinks. We've asked a speech therapist to work on getting you talking again."

My mom patted my arm in an attempt to reassure me.

My father continued. "But you are recovering very well. The driver of the other car, her name is Carol Ann."

So that's who Carol Ann is! She was in the wreck.

"She is a year younger than you and lives in the next county. Anyway, the point is, she was texting a simple message, two words, according to the report. She said the setting sun was in her eyes when she looked back up at the road. At that point, it was too late. She said she was headed right toward your car and couldn't stop. Luckily, she wasn't hurt too badly and was released from the hospital after two days."

A car hit me head-on? Some person texting a simple message? Two words? My car rolled over. I was trapped? I remembered none of this. It was as if I had amnesia of most of the time since that day.

"So, you see, son," my father continued, "this attorney, Mr. Keller, believes that we can go to court to receive some money to help with your treatment and medical expenses."

"And don't forget the charges against Carol Ann," Mom said.

"I think we should wait and see what Wes says about the charges when he can talk with us," Dad said.

"Go ahead and tell him," Granddad encouraged. "He needs to know what is happening."

I nodded.

"Mr. Keller told us that, in Texas, a driver who texts and causes an accident can be charged with a Class A misdemeanor. That means, if during the hearing, the court agrees, Carol Ann might end up in jail for a year and could have to pay a four-thousand-dollar fine in addition to covering your medical expenses. And, because you are missing your part-time job, she, or rather, her family might have to cover your missed wages."

What? Jail? Fines? I struggled to keep everything straight in my mind. This court stuff, the charges, and fines sounded horrible for this Carol Ann person. And *what was the simple message? Two words?*

"That seems like a lot for a sixteen-year-old girl to be charged with. What about her family?" Mom asked.

"Mr. Keller didn't tell me anything about her family or circumstances," Dad said. "I'm not sure how much he knows about her background."

A very cheerful nurse entered. "How are you doing, Wes? I heard you kept that applesauce down, so I brought you more food for lunch."

Thank goodness. I welcomed the distraction, especially since I felt hungry. I moved carefully to sit up higher in my bed.

"Let me help you," the nurse said. She moved one pillow up higher and assisted me by lifting me under my arms.

That's better.

I nodded and smiled at the nurse to thank her for helping me.

The nurse picked up the cover from the plate. "Now, let's see what we have. Ah, here, you have some chicken soup, a package of crackers, and some juice."

I guess this was something closer to real food. But it looked all the same color. Kind of blah.

"Want to help him?" the nurse asked my mom.

"Oh, sure."

TERRY OVERTON

Spoon-feeding again. From what Dad had said earlier about turning eighteen before the court hearing, I figured it must be close to my birthday. *Almost eighteen and being spoon-fed by my mother. I have to get better.*

"Let's just give this soup a try." Mom placed some in my mouth.

It was better than applesauce. It wasn't very warm, and it didn't have much taste when I rolled it around inside my mouth. But, after all, it was hospital food.

"There we go. Great! Want to try some crackers?" Mom asked.

I nodded.

The taste of the salty, toasty, crunchy cracker was an unexpected treat. I'd never had one so delicious. The taste of this simple food gave me hope. Hope things were looking better. I decided I would appreciate eating and the taste of food much more in the future.

Not long after my surprisingly scrumptious cracker, the nurse returned. She looked as determined as ever when she marched right over to my bedside.

"Are you ready to get unhooked from this?" The nurse took the tube in her hand. "We can take this stuff off. It will be better for you when you start your physical therapy treatment."

I smiled. Beginning my journey back to normal was fantastic. I prayed "normal" would include normal walking, talking, writing, everything like I did before the wreck.

"There we go. Now, let's get this tape off."

At last! Free from wires and tubes.

All the activity caught up with me, and my eyes started to close again. The nurse assisted me in getting comfortable.

Then the door opened.

In bounced in a cheerful, petite young woman in professional dress. "Hello, Wes, I'm April. I'm your speech therapist. I'll be working with you to get that communication going again. I know you want to tell us what you are thinking."

I smiled. This was the first female under twenty-five years

of age who had been in my room. I knew she was older than me, but not by much. And she was pretty! She was really pretty.

My room was a busy place, people in and out, but being able to walk and talk again would be amazing. I vowed to cooperate with April and Alex and get myself going again, no matter how hard I'd have to work.

I wanted my mouth to say the same words I thought. So far, I was able to think a word, but my mouth didn't always go along with the thought. When I made a word, the sounds were different than I remembered.

April asked the nurse, "Is he eating solid foods?"

"Almost there. He ate soup today and chewed a cracker."

"Excellent. Let me see you take a sip of your juice with your straw."

I carefully sipped the cold, sweet beverage through the straw.

"There. Looks like your speech muscles are moving okay here. You're able to swallow, move your lips, use a straw, and I understand you have uttered a few words. We'll investigate thoroughly tomorrow afternoon. We'll work on strengthening your muscles and breathing for talking. I wanted to stop in and meet you today. I'll be back tomorrow after lunch. Sound good?"

I nodded. I looked forward to seeing her again. She was like a breath of fresh air, a sign of hope for me returning back to my life.

Now, exhaustion overwhelmed me. I could no longer keep my eyes open. I dozed off between the nurses who came in and out.

"Wes, why don't you get some rest? I will be back early tomorrow before your physical therapy," Granddad said. Then he leaned over and whispered, "And I'll bring you a donut hole or two."

He picked up my hand and gave it a tight squeeze, then hugged me.

I smiled and fell asleep the moment he left the room.

CHAPTER SEVENTEEN

The Long Road Back

The sun crashed into the room from the window and blasted all the way through my closed eyelids. A nurse had opened the curtains as wide as they would go and then scurried around the room preparing everything for my sponge bath. I dreaded the sponge bath but was grateful afterward.

"Not long now, and you'll be getting into the shower on your own. But don't worry, once you start moving around, I will get Phil or Juan to help you. You'll need a male nurse until you get your balance back. Not sure I could catch you if you started to fall."

That was good news. Having a nurse give you a sponge bath is humiliating enough. I welcomed getting a male nurse to help me.

The changing of my sheets followed my routine sponge bath. The assistant with my breakfast tray came in. And right behind the assistant, Granddad walked in holding a small white bag in one hand that bumped against his walker. I knew what was inside—delicious donut holes Jae had made just this morning.

Granddad held his finger up to his mouth, whispered "Shh...," and winked at me. He placed the small white bag in his jacket pocket.

"Good morning, Wes," Granddad smiled.

The nurse checked my vitals, made sure everything was okay, and then spun the bedside tray across my lap. She lifted the cover off the plate and there were fluffy yellow scrambled eggs.

Real food. I smiled.

"Sir, would you like to help him out with these eggs?"

"Yes, of course."

Granddad made his way over and steadied his walker against his chair. "Now, let's see here, son. These look pretty good." Granddad picked up the fork and scooped some up to give me. "Oh, and they are still warm. Even better. You have orange juice here. I'll put the straw in for you, buddy."

Granddad helped me eat a few bites of the scrambled egg. "Is it okay for him to have coffee?"

"Yes, I will get some for him. Cream and sugar?"

"No, he takes it black. Thank you."

The nurse returned with the coffee. "Mr. Williams, we are slowly reducing his medication for pain. He might start to get his appetite back."

"Good to hear."

"Yes, so, if you like, you can give him a bite or two of what you brought in that white bag you stuffed in your pocket." She laughed.

Granddad chuckled and winked at me. "Busted me again."

Granddad took the bag from his pocket and placed a donut hole on the plate. He cut the donut hole in half and placed a bite in my mouth. Even before the donut hole landed on my tongue, my mouth watered.

Tastes like a bite of heaven. I smiled. Then I thought a bite of heaven was close to the truth. The Donut Shop had been my place in my own near-death Heaven experience. I wanted desperately to tell my grandfather about what had happened. I wanted to ask about Jae, Old Walt, Parker, and Lawson. I wanted to tell him I saw Jimmy again and remind him of all the stories and jokes we shared when I was younger.

Determined, I moved my mouth as much as possible.

"Wes, do you want to tell me something?" Granddad asked.

I nodded.

"Want me to guess?"

I nodded. Could he possibly know my thoughts? *Donut Shop! Donut Shop!*

"Is it something about the donuts?"

I nodded again.

"Is it about the flavor? Or did you want a cake donut or bear claw?"

I shook my head no.

"Let me see, something about the Donut Shop but not the food?"

I nodded yes. *The guys—Old Walt, Parker, Lawson.*

"Okay. Maybe the people? The guys at the shop?"

I nodded.

"How about I bring them around in a few days? Would you like to see them?"

I smiled.

"I will talk it over with them tomorrow and see when we can all come in at the same time. I'm sure they would like to see you."

Another large smile emerged across my face. I put the words "thank you" in my mind and moved them into my mouth. *Work, mouth!*

"Tha–"

"You're welcome, son."

You understood me! And you will ask them to visit.

For a moment, the thought of being back with the guys from the Donut Shop filled me with a warm glow inside, like it did when I'd visited during my near-death experience.

"Oh, I almost forgot." Granddad reached into his other pocket and retrieved a small wooden block. He sat it on the bed table.

I turned my head and silently read the writing on the block. *"I can do all things through him who strengthens me," Philippians 4:13.*

Uncontrollable tears filled my eyes

"I thought this might help us get through your therapy together." He smiled.

I nodded. It was the most perfect gift he could have given me.

My parents walked in just as Granddad fed me another bite of the donut hole.

"Is he supposed to eat that?" Mom asked.

"Nurse said he could."

Granddad and I both smiled. Each bite took me back there. I hoped to see Granddad's buddies from the Donut Shop in the next day or two. I prayed they would want to come visit me.

"Hi, Wes," Alex said as he entered the room. "Looks like you ate a good breakfast. And the tubes are gone! Wow, that's a milestone. Now, let's work on getting you stronger. First things first. Are you ready to stand up?"

Fear overcame me all the way to the pit of my stomach. My face felt pale, and I knew Alex detected my anxiety. I glanced at the block beside my bed. *"I can do all things through him who strengthens me," Philippians 4:13.*

"Don't worry. I'll hold on to you. We must get started sometime. Might as well be today. You ready?"

My grandfather scooted his chair away from my bed. "You can finish eating the other one later." He winked. "If you stand up."

Alex lowered my bed, so it was closer to the floor. He helped me sit up by placing his hands and arms under my arms as support. Then he helped me swing my legs around so my feet were on the floor. "Now, steady. I want you to slowly place the weight on your feet and legs and try to straighten...yes...that's right. There you go."

What an incredible feeling. I was no longer on my back. I stood on my own two feet. But standing added a new sensation. I felt myself sway slightly, and my eyes struggled to focus as the room started spinning. I silently repeated, *"I can do all things through him who strengthens me."*

"Now, let's just stand here a moment. Feeling okay?"

I slowly nodded. *Not really, but no way am I getting back in that bed already.*

"See this chair? It's about two steps away. I'm going to hold on to you and walk with you to the chair. We'll see if you can sit in the chair for a few minutes."

The progress was slow. It took mammoth effort to make my stronger leg lift off the floor and place my foot slightly closer to the chair. Then, with as little weight as possible, I placed my right leg with the cast lightly on the floor and then shifted back to the left leg. One slow foot at a time. One huge effort. A tiny bit of progress. Then another step.

"Good. There, you've got this. Good. Now, slowly, let's sit down on the chair. Careful, careful."

My body core quivered. I felt unsteady. Again, my mind repeated the Scripture: *"I can do all things through him who strengthens me."*

"You are doing fine. Nearly there. Okay. There."

I did it! I was sitting in a chair. No longer in the bed.

"I'll let you sit here for a while. I will be back in a few minutes, but," he glanced toward my grandfather, "if you need me, ring the nurse and I'll get you back into bed. You okay?"

I nodded.

"You look better sitting up," Granddad said and smiled.

I smiled.

Granddad relayed the news from his latest visit to the Donut Shop. Jae had at last hired someone else to work in the shop with her. "Yeah, she said business was good, and she was getting tired of being the only one working in the shop."

I nodded.

"The new guy at the shop is named Li. He's Jae's nephew and seems to be a hard worker. He caught on quickly. She told me he is learning how to make the donuts. Of course, he has to report to work at four-thirty each morning."

Four-thirty? That's early. Since I could not tell Granddad what I thought, I could only open my eyes with shock.

"I know, that is early," Granddad said.

He knows my feelings and what I'm thinking. Guess he knows me pretty well.

Twenty minutes later, Alex came back and helped me to bed.

"You are on the road to recovery. We'll work on a few more things tomorrow. In a day or so, we will have you walking around in the hallways using a trainer to lean on and help you build up your balance and strength. Mom, if you want to bring him his pajamas and bathrobe, it might be better for the hallway. Or you can bring him a set of sweats to wear when we go down to the physical therapy room."

The look of surprise on my face was detected right away.

"Oh yes, we'll be going to the other room and put you on a treadmill kind of thing. We'll get you stronger. Don't worry. You're doing great."

I smiled again. Next, I had to get my speech back. Then I'd tell my grandfather everything. And I'd talk to my parents about the wreck and Carol Ann. I had a lot of questions. I wondered about the two words in the message Carol Ann felt she had to send. What was so urgent? Why did she need to text while she was driving on the road that night?

CHAPTER EIGHTEEN

Words, Conversations, and A Spoon

My grandfather and father left shortly after Alex helped me back into the hospital bed. Mom stayed to help me eat my lunch. *God, please help me feed myself one day soon.*

"Here's you some lunch," the patient assistant said.

"Thank you, Miss," my mother said. "Let's take a look. Hmm...I think this is stew. Yes, there are carrots, potatoes, and beef. And you have a roll, pudding, and juice. Looks almost like solid food. Pretty close."

I smiled. I ate the most food I had eaten since, well, I didn't know how long. But it tasted better than it looked and that was a good thing. It looked disgusting.

My day had been busy already, and I knew I needed a nap. I couldn't hold my eyes open another minute. Dad and Mom said their goodbyes and told me they'd be back later. I drifted to sleep, but like every day since I'd been out of the coma, my sleep was interrupted. April, smiling and looking quite charming, opened the door. Along with her came a man I had not met.

"Wes, this is Lorenzo."

"Nice to meet you, bud," he said, extending his hand. He picked my hand up from the bed and shook it. "I'm your occupational therapist or OT for short."

I smiled, tried to shake his hand, and nodded.

"Let me check out your hands and see what's going on."

Lorenzo moved both of my hands, fingers, wrists, and arms. He then gave me several commands to use my hands to do things, to reach, to try and point, and to stretch out my arms. I tried very hard to do what he asked, but I felt weak.

"Okay, buddy. Looks like we will need to build up this strength. Now, for feeding yourself..."

Yes! I want to do that, please.

"We have an adaptive spoon you can use for a bit. I don't want you to get used to it. I think you will hold a regular spoon after we get you stronger. The doctor told you about the swelling in your brain?"

I nodded.

"He thinks the swelling is temporary, and it's getting better. You're going to get another CT scan today and we can see about your progress. The more the swelling goes down, the better you will be. You should be able to get your motor skills back. But we will take it slowly. I'll be back at dinnertime, and we can see about you working on feeding yourself with the spoon I'll bring you." He turned toward April. "Okay, April, I'll leave him with you."

I nodded and smiled. I wanted to do everything as I had before. Most of all, I wanted to talk. I looked at April and hoped she could help me.

"Let's have a look inside your mouth and check out your tongue and see how everything is functioning."

April placed a tongue depressor in my mouth and looked around inside with a light. Then she used some type of thing that felt like rubber. She gave me commands to move, bite, and swallow.

"Okay, it looks pretty good inside. Now, let's check your memory. I have a book here with pictures. Each page has four pictures. I will say a word, then you can nod when I point to the picture of that word. If I point to the wrong word, you won't do anything. So, on this page, if I said 'apple' and then point to this picture of the car, what would you do?"

I did nothing.

"Okay, good. You do nothing. Now when I say apple and then point to the apple, you will..."

I nodded.

"Perfect. Let's go through this. These may get harder as we

go, and it is okay if I say a word and you don't know the answer. Okay?"

I nodded.

The evaluation was like a game. The words and pictures weren't hard until the last few pages. I figured I remembered most of the words.

"Good job, Wes. Good news. Looks like you remembered about ninety-five percent of the names of these pictures. Tomorrow, we will see if you can tell when I use the words correctly in sentences. And we will get you to use whatever speech sounds you can. Soon, we will give the muscles in your mouth a workout and I will ask to make some sounds. It will all get easier as the brain swelling goes down. Sound good?"

I nodded.

"Now I'll let you get back to your nap." April winked, then turned to leave.

I nodded. I thought April was very sweet as well as pretty. She had shoulder-length reddish hair and green eyes. I looked forward to our sessions together. I knew I would make progress and be speaking again. I *must* learn to talk again.

No sooner did I fall asleep, and my afternoon nap was interrupted again.

An assistant entered the room with a wheelchair. "Hi, Wes. I'm here to take you down for more scans."

Another nurse followed the assistant into my room. They quickly lowered my bed and helped me into the wheelchair. They took me down the hallway to the elevator. It was the first time since my surgery I had been out of my hospital room. Or perhaps the first time I could remember being out of the room. It was exciting to see other people, even if most were hospital staff.

The tests weren't difficult to endure and soon the attendant and the nurse placed me back in my bed. I expected dinner any minute and Lorenzo would appear with his special type of spoon. And he did.

"Hey, Wes," Lorenzo said from the doorway. "Oh, food not here yet? I'll go out and get it for you."

Mom and Dad returned to my room.

"Hi, Wes. I brought you some of your clothes," Mom said. "Here are a couple of pairs of sweatpants and tee-shirts, your pajamas, and robe. They didn't mention shoes, but I brought these, and some socks."

Mom looked down at my cast and added, "Well, maybe you can wear your left shoe."

Looking at Mom I muttered, "Tha–."

"You're welcome."

I smiled because Mom understood what I said, or rather, what I meant.

"Ready to eat dinner? They should bring it in about now," Mom said.

I nodded.

Lorenzo returned with dinner and introduced himself to my parents. "And now, Wes, here's your dinner tray. Oh, and here is the spoon for you to try. I'll help you until you get the hang of it."

Lorenzo opened a package with a blue spoon that reminded me of a baby spoon. It looked like it was made of rubber.

"Now, the point of this spoon," he paused and looked at my parents, "is so he won't cut his lip trying to eat with a metal spoon or fork. It will take practice. He should get the hang of it pretty quick, though. And then we can use a regular spoon. Ready to try?"

I nodded.

Mom took the cover from the plate of food. "Maybe...meatloaf? I'm not sure. And mashed potatoes."

Lorenzo placed the spoon in my hand. I held it loosely and was afraid it would fall. But Lorenzo kept his hand on mine and helped me hold on to the spoon. I scooped up some food and moved the spoon toward my mouth. I couldn't help but smile. I fed myself mashed potatoes. *I'm eating!*

I thought back for a moment to the things I'd done so far in high school. I'd made good grades, won a couple of track meets, but this accomplishment was better than all that. I knew this accomplishment meant I would gain independence back.

The door opened and in stepped the doctor.

"Hello, Wes, and Mr. and Mrs. Williams. Good to see you sitting up, Wes. Hi, Lorenzo, Got that fellow eating?"

"Yes sir. Doing really good."

"Wes, I've known you for several weeks, but it occurred to me you might not know my name because, well, we weren't properly introduced in the emergency room." He laughed. "I'm Doctor Arnold."

I nodded.

"I reviewed the report from your scans today. They show marked improvement compared to the scans from last week. You are one lucky fellow. I will write up the orders for continued therapies. We will look at things again in a few days. We might get you moved to a rehab center or, if you continue to make great progress, we can get you home."

This was the best thing Dr. Arnold could have said. Home. I couldn't wait to get back there.

CHAPTER NINETEEN

The Donut Gang

Since I continued to feel stronger and showed improvement every day, Mom and Dad decided to return to work and visit me in the afternoons. I was now kind of feeding myself and had been gaining strength in my legs, even with my injury. My therapy evaluations indicated I'd made marked progress in the last few days. I felt hopeful.

Yesterday, my daily sponge bath had been replaced by a real shower. Okay, well, not quite a real shower yet. I sat in a plastic shower chair in the shower. All seventeen years of my life, I had overlooked how glorious it was to be in a shower and feel the warm water dripping on my head and down my back. Feeling the soapsuds lathered all over was magnificent. Definitely a huge improvement over sponge baths.

Getting in the shower had been a task. Phil, one of my assistants, helped me slowly shuffle to the bathroom. After I was safely seated in the shower chair, he wrapped plastic around my cast to keep it dry. Afterward, we made the slow shuffle to the chair in my room, and Phil changed my sheets before letting me back in bed for a nap.

Taking that shower yesterday was perfect because, today, at last, I would see the people I wanted to see the most. The guys from the Donut Shop were coming by and bringing me breakfast.

"Okay, Wes, let's get you dressed for your company. How many are coming in this group?" Juan, my assistant this morning, asked. He grabbed a set of sweats and laid them on the table.

My mouth moved to say four, but "fur" is what came out.

"Okay. Uh, four?"

I nodded.

"Good. Four is a good size group in this small room. After we get you dressed and you get back on the bed, I'll bring in a couple of extra chairs, okay?"

I nodded. Juan helped me put my clean clothes on and then he combed my hair. Every chance I had, I looked at the clock. I was excited. I hoped someday I could communicate to the men how much they meant to me and how I have missed them.

Granddad opened the door and entered, pushing his walker. Parker, Old Walt, and Lawson followed. I immediately missed seeing Jimmy, who had made been alive in my near-death experience.

"There's my boy," Granddad said. He scooted in and hugged me.

"Hey Wes," Old Walt said. "You look like you're taking it easy." Old Walt came to the other side of my bed and hugged me.

Lawson appeared to be a little bothered, and I hoped I didn't look too bad to him. "Wes" was all he said as he leaned over to hug me.

Parker moved a chair aside and hugged me as the others had done. I felt a wonderful warmth with each hug. Parker, who was always quiet, had a longer greeting than Lawson, and that was a first. Parker said, "Wes, when your grandfather told me about the wreck, I said, 'That young man is a fighter. He can do anything he sets his mind to.'"

Juan brought in the two extra chairs and the men took their seats.

"Here you are," Granddad said, placing the donuts on a paper plate. "Two glazed and one chocolate covered. And a cup of hot coffee. Jae fixed these up just as you like them."

I smiled. I could not control the tears filling my eyes. I was overcome with gratefulness with the blessing of knowing these men.

"Well now, Wes, I knew you really liked Jae's donuts." He smiled and dabbed the tears off my cheeks.

"H–"

"Yes, what is it?"

I took in a breath, moved my mouth, breathed out at the same time, and said, "Hi."

"Goodness! He said 'Hi' plain as day, fellas. Good for you, Wes." Granddad grinned. He understood what I'd just accomplished.

I smiled bigger than Texas. It was my first easily understood word. I *was* making headway.

"You been behaving yourself in here?" Lawson smiled. "Wouldn't want you causing any trouble."

I smiled and nodded.

Granddad cut up my donut and helped me scoop up the pieces in my spoon. Then he said, "You know what, Wes? Let's just see if you can get these pieces all on your own."

I'd had a couple of days of practice and could bring the pieces of donuts all the way to my mouth. I knew it wouldn't be long before I was doing more on my own. It just took practice.

"Well," Old Walt said, "the whole gang is here. We figured you needed to hear some stories."

Granddad started off with the jokes. "Yes, let's talk about our visits to the hospital. Parker, let's start with you."

"Never been to the hospital," Parker replied.

Granddad wagged his finger at Parker. "That's not true at all."

"What are you talking about? I would remember something like that," Parker insisted.

"You have been to the hospital just as sure as I'm sittin' here."

"You must be thinking of someone else."

"Nope." Granddad shook his head.

"I've never been in the hospital."

"Where are you now?" Granddad tried to hide his grin behind his hand.

Parker chuckled. "You got me."

A knock on the door interrupted our laughter. Dr. Arnold poked his head in. "Wes, this is quite a gathering here. Hello, Mr.

Williams, good to see you again."

"And you, sir," my grandfather said.

"I know Wes is enjoying all of this company. Wes, is it okay to speak among your Granddad and friends?"

I nodded, and he walked to the foot of my bed

"Good. I have been going over all your records. We have a decision to make. You, your grandfather, and parents can talk this over. You are making terrific progress. The swelling we were worried about is just nearly gone and, well, you are recuperating at a fairly rapid rate. We can continue to keep you here a couple more days, run one more scan to be sure everything is improving, and then send you home. Or you can go this afternoon to a rehab facility if you prefer. Just think about it and have your parents talk it over. You would probably want to have someone with you at your house, and we can talk about outpatient therapy if you decide to go home."

This was terrific news! I wanted to be back in my own room and my own house. To be in familiar surroundings, to smell the smells of the kitchen when Mom cooks dinner, to have people over to visit. That's what I wanted. I hoped it would be the same plan my parents wanted for me.

"Thank you, Dr. Arnold," Granddad said. "I can stay with him at his house during the day while his parents work if he goes home. And I can drive him to therapy sessions."

Dr. Arnold made a note on the paper in his hand, "That would work if that is what you all want to do."

I nodded and smiled. "Tha–yo."

"That was great! You are talking more," Granddad said and patted my arm.

"I'll be back around this evening and see what you all plan."

"Now, where were we?" Granddad asked as the door closed behind Dr. Arnold. "Oh yes, Parker's time at the hospital."

We all laughed, and the jokes continued. It was such fun to hear the stories and see these guys having a good time together. I wished they would stay all day and return every day.

A knock on the door was followed by a woman's voice. "Is

this Wes Williams's room?" The door slowly opened.

I know that voice.

"Wes?"

Old Walt said, "Jae! How did you escape from the Donut Shop?"

"You silly guy. I own shop. I tell Li to stay at shop and I come here. I want to see for myself," she said.

I knew my smile beamed across my face. It felt like a homecoming. Granddad and his friends and even Jae came.

"Wes," Jae laughed, "I not want you to deal with all these old guys alone. They are mess!"

We all laughed.

I uttered, "Yes."

"My boy! You are getting your speech back! Wonderful!"

"He has to be able to talk to put up with the likes of you," Lawson said.

"I suppose that's about right," Granddad agreed.

Jae stayed a short time, and the others left one by one. I hoped, next time we got together, it would be at the Donut Shop on a Saturday. Just like we used to do before the wreck.

Granddad left last. Before leaving, he hugged me and said, "Tell your folks to call me. We can talk about what you want to do."

"Tha–yo."

"See, you are talking more each day. That's fine, son. I will see you tomorrow morning, and I'll bring you some donuts."

I felt worn out from the excitement. I knew I had therapy scheduled for later in the day. I'd be moving down the hallway in the mobility trainer designed to help me learn to walk again. As eager as I was to learn, I knew the exercise would be tiring. I let myself doze off for a bit, but an unfamiliar voice interrupted my nap before I was ready to wake up.

"Wes? Are you Wes Williams?" a girl's voice said.

I woke to see a girl I did not know standing in the doorway. I nodded.

"Hello, Wes. I'm...I'm Carol Ann."

CHAPTER TWENTY

Carol Ann

At first, I imagined I was dreaming. I had been in a deep sleep and believed I still was. I sat up, looked, and focused my eyes. This stranger at the door looked angelic. Her hair fell in curls down upon her shoulders. Her small silver earrings dangled from her ears. She was dressed in a simple white blouse, and a single silver chain with a cross hung around her neck. The blouse flowed gently over her slacks and a small purse hung on her shoulder. She was real. She was beautiful, and I was awake.

"I am so sorry to wake you."

I didn't know how to reply since I had few words that would make it from my brain to my mouth. I moved my hand and motioned for her to come inside.

"Do you know who I am?"

I looked at her but was unable to reply.

A black hand brace emerged from the long white sleeve that covered her right arm, but otherwise, she looked to be in good health with no problems after the wreck. In her other hand, she held something that looked like a small book.

She meekly walked into the room, approached the side of the bed, and placed her hand on the back of the chair. "May I sit?"

I nodded.

"Are you able to talk? I mean, can you speak?"

I shook my head. I could make sounds, but I didn't consider it speaking, especially not with a stranger.

Carol Ann looked down. It was clear to me she looked distraught. "Wes, I understand you were extensively injured. I know it was my fault. I know I am the reason you are here. I know I caused the wreck."

She sat silently and cried. Several minutes passed. I felt helpless and not able to do anything. She collected her emotions and continued, "I came to tell you I'm sorry. I am so very sorry." Her tears started again. She put her head down on the bed and sobbed. Her head and shoulders quivered with the weight of sorrow she must feel.

My heart was sad for her. I could tell she was full of remorse. More than ever, I needed speech. I needed to tell her I was not angry or upset. I wanted her to know everything would be okay. I was getting better and growing stronger.

She attempted to compose herself once again. She took a handful of tissues from my night table. "Sorry, I didn't bring any tissues with me."

I reached over to her hand and nodded to let her know she was fine. I didn't want her to be upset about anything else.

She remained quiet and picked up the book she'd placed next to her on the chair. "I wanted to give this to you."

She placed the book in my hand, and I held it as firmly as I was able. I looked at the cover. "Holy Bible" was barely visible on the black cracked cover.

"It is a Bible that my grandfather had with him in the Korean War. He was a Marine. He was in a battle one time and was almost killed. Many of the men he was with were killed that day. This little Bible was small enough for his pocket. Before he passed away, he told me he believed this little Bible kept him safe during war times and throughout the rest of his life. He was a man of strong faith. He wanted me to share the story about this Bible with someone that I wanted to keep safe. And, after what happened..." Her voice trailed off, and she started to cry once again.

I patted her on her arm and then held her hand. I wished I could tell her my own grandfather was in the same war. I wondered if my grandfather knew her grandfather since we only lived one county over. Maybe someday I would be able to talk to Granddad about her grandfather when my speech returned.

"Wes, I know you might not feel like doing this right now, but I have prayed every single day since the accident that God would make you well again and keep you alive so I could talk to you. I have prayed that someday I'd be able to ask for your forgiveness. I prayed I'd be able to make it up to you."

She brushed her hair away from her eyes and said, "Last night, I had a dream. It was so real. When I woke up, I believed it had happened. My grandfather...my grandfather died two years ago." Her voice cracked with emotion. "Last night, in my dream, he was at my house. It was as real as you and me sitting here right at this moment. He told me to bring this Bible to you."

My eyes teared up. I felt as if I knew her grandfather and how hard the war probably was for him. I knew how strong he was in his faith, like my own grandfather. Even though I'd never met this man, I could sense I knew him somehow.

"Can you ever...Can you find it in your heart to forgive me? Just think about it. Maybe someday you can?"

I patted her hand and nodded. I knew I had already forgiven her.

She stood up and pulled her car keys out of her purse. "May I come back to see you? If you don't want me to, I understand."

I held her hand and nodded.

"It's okay, then?"

I nodded again. I wanted her to tell me about the short message she'd texted, the message that resulted in my totaled car and banged up body and head. I held up two fingers.

Carol Ann shrugged her shoulders. I wanted to ask her to tell me the two words she felt so important that she had to text and drive.

I gestured to her phone again.

"My phone? Something about my phone?"

I nodded. I tried to make the motions with my thumbs as if I were texting. I held up two fingers again.

She hung her head again. "You are asking me about the text? The two words." She sat back down and stared at her phone for a few seconds. I feared her tears would start again. She sat up straight and looked at me, and I could see determination in her expression. Her lips quivered as she murmured, "Running late."

I was shocked. Such a simple message. Such a short time to take her eyes off the road. In just a few seconds, both of our lives changed.

She continued, "I was going home. I was running late, and it was a school night. I promised my parents I would be home before dark, and the sun was setting."

Tears fell silently down her cheeks, and she wiped them away with a tissue.

I thought about her message for a moment. I knew I had done the same thing before. I knew I had texted when I was driving. I knew I had texted my parents and friends the same message whenever I was running late. Feeling sorry that she was in so much mental anguish, I took her hand and squeezed.

We sat for a few more moments, holding hands in the silence. Then she squeezed my hand and stood up. "May I hug you before I leave?"

I nodded.

"I will see you in a few days, Wes." She paused and smiled faintly. "Thank you."

I smiled and nodded.

Carol Ann left my room as quietly as she entered. I might have thought I dreamed it all except for the tiny Bible still in my hand. I opened the cover with my thumb and saw handwritten letters inside. The first line, written in faded blue ink, said, "Heavenly Father, thank you for bringing me back home safely from Korea."

The next line, written in the same handwriting and a bolder blue ink, said, "To my granddaughter Carol Ann. May this keep you safe. Pass it on if someone you know and care for needs protection."

The third line, written in black ink and a girl's handwriting, said, "To Wes, may God protect you always, Carol Ann."

My heart was full of many emotions all at once. I read the writing several times, each time it felt more meaningful.

After lunch, I participated in my usual therapy sessions and felt I was making great gains. In speech therapy, I practiced forcing the air out powerfully enough to make sounds, but it was difficult. For OT, Lorenzo had me practicing putting my arms through my shirt and pulling on my sweatpants. But by late afternoon, when my parents arrived after work, I was worn out. It had been a full day, and while my physical therapy session was challenging, I knew I made more progress.

"Hey, Son," Dad said when he came in with Mom.

"H–h–hi." I smiled when the word came out.

"Wow! Well done!" Dad grinned. "You're making good progress."

"What's this?" Mom picked up the small Bible on my table. She opened it and read the writing on the inside cover. "Carol Ann was here? I asked her last week not to come yet."

I smiled. I wanted to let Mom know it was going to be okay. I took a breath and, with every effort I could make, I said, "O...kay"

Dad grinned again. "Did you hear that? He's talking up a storm!"

I let out a small chuckle.

"You think it was okay that she came by?" Mom asked.

I tried to say "yes" but decided the "y" sound was too hard. I nodded instead.

"Does she realize what she did? Running you off the road like that? Texting and driving?"

Attempting to calm Mom down, Dad said, "If it is okay with Wes, then we should accept her coming by."

I nodded again. Then I tried once more to sound out a new word, hoping my parents knew what I meant. "So...r."

"Are you saying sorry?" Dad asked.

I nodded.

"Sorry...hmm...you mean she was sorry?" Dad looked puzzled.

I nodded.

"Carol Ann said she was sorry? She came by to say she was sorry?"

I nodded.

Dad frowned. "I wanted to talk to her."

This comment from Dad disturbed me, but I was not able to elaborate on how upset Carol Ann was, how much she cried. I knew she understood the wreck was entirely her fault. But I also realized I had been guilty of texting while driving. It could have easily been me texting and not her.

An assistant interrupted our conversation and placed my dinner tray on my table. Mom uncovered the plate, and her expression told me she had no clue what was on the plate. "Hmmm. What do you think, Wes?"

Dad looked at the food. "Ugh. What is that stuff? I'll tell you what I think of this food. I think I'll go down the street and pick us all up some burgers. We can eat together."

I beamed. Real food. My mouth watered at the thought. And my burger tasted better than I could ever have imagined.

CHAPTER TWENTY-ONE

Determination

The next day felt full of resolve. I was determined to get out of this place. I wanted to get out sooner rather than later. Enough was enough. I was wide awake when the first nurse opened my door to check me over.

"You're up early today."

"Ye–" was my attempt to say yes. At least it was more than the day before.

"Oh! And chatting already." She smiled as she pulled the curtains open.

Today, it didn't bother me when the light poured in. I welcomed it. The day seemed different. I was full of willpower. I would talk as much as possible all day. I would work harder with Alex, Lorenzo, and April. I would do more than they asked. I wanted to go home.

"There's my boy," Granddad said. He arrived earlier than usual and scooted in with his walker and the familiar white bag bouncing on its side. When he came alone, there was no way he could manage my coffee.

"Say, miss," he said to the nurse, "would you be able to bring in two cups of coffee?"

"Yes sir. Any cream or sugar?"

"No, thank you. Both black."

She hastily departed.

"I phoned in the order and picked up both of our usual donuts. Thought I'd eat with you today. The gang hadn't even arrived at the Donut Shop when I drove up to the pickup window."

I smiled. "Tha you."

"Now that sounded amazing! You are getting better each day. Just remember..." He gestured toward the small wood block with the verse on it and read the words, *"I can do all things through him who strengthens me."*

I nodded. I desperately wanted to tell him about Carol Ann. I vowed to think of a way to let him know.

Returning with our coffees, the nurse put them on the tray and swung the tray over my bed. "Here you go."

"Thank you," Granddad said. He went to the sink and took out some paper towels. "These look like the perfect plates."

I laughed.

"Now, there you go. Two glazed and one chocolate. Oh, Jae said to tell you hello. And Li. He wants to meet you. I told him it wouldn't be too much longer. Once you're at home, I can pick you up."

I nodded. I was still amazed that Granddad, in his early eighties, walker and all, could drive and get around. He simply folded up his walker and tossed it in the back of the car. I was thankful he was able to get around town.

Granddad took his first bite. "Now, oh, the bear claw is always perfect."

I tentatively picked up the donut in my hand to eat it. No need to cut it into pieces. Last night, I'd eaten my burger like normal. I made a mess with it, but it felt good to be eating like a regular person. We ate in silence for a few minutes.

After my second donut, I wondered if I could write. I had not tried that yet. But today, I decided I would try. Maybe I could communicate to Granddad what I wanted. I moved my hand in a writing motion as if I were holding a pencil.

"You want something? A pencil?"

"Ye–"

"I'll get you one."

Granddad scooted his walker to the door and stuck his head out and saw an assistant in the hallway. "Say, Miss, would you be able to bring us a paper and pencil?"

"Yes sir."

He scooted back to his chair. "That pretty assistant will get us fixed up." He winked.

The donuts were as delicious as always. The hospital coffee was so-so, certainly not as good as Jae's coffee. I longed for the day when I could go to the Donut Shop myself. I hoped it wouldn't be too long.

The door opened, and the assistant popped in. "Here you go, sir."

"Thank you. Now, Wes, want to give it a try?" He moved the paper towels, covered with the remaining donut crumbs, aside. He held the paper down so it wouldn't move as I attempted to write.

I took the pencil in my hand. I had trouble gripping it and dropped it a couple of times on the tray. I was determined to write this time. I scribbled a C. It even looked like a C. But it resembled a letter a first grader might write.

"C," Granddad acknowledged it, and I was happy he knew what it was

It was difficult to write my letters the usual size. I know now why first-grade writing looks primitive. I couldn't make my letters small. At last, I wrote a large A.

"A," Granddad said. He watched every stroke of the pencil and called out each letter.

At last, I finished writing her first name.

"Carol?" Granddad asked.

"Ye–"

I motioned my hand to indicate the idea of her being "here."

"Someone named Carol was here?" he asked.

I nodded and started my attempt to write "Ann." I had only completed the first letter when Granddad stopped me.

"Carol Ann? Carol Ann was here? She came to see you?"

"Ye–" I smiled.

"How was that?"

I smiled.

"Were your parents here when she came by?"

"N–n–" I murmured.

"Oh. Was her visit, uh, okay?"

"Ye–"

I picked up the pencil again and struggled to write the letter *S*. I managed to write out *s-o-r* before Granddad stopped me again. "Sorry? She said she was sorry?"

"Ye–"

Granddad took the last bite of his bear claw and seemed to be thinking about what I had just told him. "How do you feel about that, son?"

I smiled. I didn't know how to get the details across to him. The paper was just about covered with the large letters I had written. I turned the page over. I scribbled what I hoped looked like a lowercase *G*. I had finished the letters *g-o-o* when Granddad guessed.

"Good? You felt good? Glad to hear it, Wes. Was she, uh, let's see, was she sincere you think?"

I nodded and smiled.

"Well, that's fine. I am glad to hear that you felt good about whatever she said to you. When you are up to it, maybe you can tell me more about her visit."

"Ye–"

My parents opened the door just then, and they were not alone. A man I didn't know accompanied them.

"Good morning, Wes," my dad said.

"Hi, Honey," Mom said as she leaned over to kiss my forehead.

"Mor–," I replied.

"Oh, terrific!" Mom said. "Did you hear Wes? He tried to say 'morning' back to me. Good job, Honey."

"Yes," Dad replied. "Wes, I'd like you to meet someone. This is Mr. Keller. He wanted to say hi before he went into the office today. He is your attorney."

I nodded.

At that exact moment, Phil came through the door. "Oh, I see you have company. I will come back in a few minutes to get you to the shower."

I nodded.

"I will be talking to you a lot in the future, Wes." Mr. Keller had a deep voice. "I want to find out exactly what happened and your experience. I've looked over the accident investigation report, your medical records, and the statements from Carol Ann. We will go from there."

I nodded.

"Well, I won't keep you," Mr. Keller continued. "Just wanted to meet you. We will have plenty of time to talk before I file with the court."

I didn't know what all of that meant. I wanted to know, but I also wanted to stall Mr. Keller until I had more speech and could talk to him. I wanted to explain to him how I felt and that I didn't want to punish Carol Ann. She had suffered enough already. I didn't see the point in putting her through more agony.

"Thank you, Mr. Keller, for coming by," Dad said. The men shook hands, and Mr. Keller left.

Granddad wasted no time telling my parents what I had written.

"Wes was able to write this morning! He said Carol Ann came by and said she was sorry."

"Yes, he told us yesterday after she left," Dad replied.

"Are you going to wait until Wes can talk more before you go to court?" Granddad asked.

"Yes." Mom straightened my blanket. "We want him to tell the court what has happened to him."

I thought about Mom's words. There was no way, even if I had all my speech back, to fully convey what had happened to me. Words could not adequately tell people what being near death was like. As terrifying as it might have sounded to me before the wreck, somehow now, having been through it myself, my thinking had changed.

My parents, and Granddad included, didn't know the experience had changed my life in so many ways. Somehow, I needed to be able to describe it—the sensation of seeing yourself at death's door, the comfort I felt when I heard His voice as He told me I would live, the joy I felt seeing Jimmy alive and Granddad not yet disabled, and the warmth I felt as I heard those amazing stories once again that I had heard years ago. It was indescribable. I knew I had to try to explain it all someday.

CHAPTER TWENTY-TWO

Little by Little

Mom and Dad didn't stay long since they both had to get to work. They promised to return later. Granddad stayed a few more minutes until Phil returned.

"Hey, Wes, ready for your shower?"

"Ye–" I said.

"I'll leave you two to get at that. Now, Wes, I will come back later if you'd like."

Of course, I would. I always want you to come by. "Ye–," I said.

"Say around four? Or wait, I will come a little later and bring you something for dinner."

There was no doubt he understood my joy at that suggestion. My face had a smile plastered from ear to ear.

"Okay, then. I'll pick something up. I'll let your folks know."

I nodded.

"Goodbye, Mr. Williams. Good to see you," Phil said. "Now, let's get you going."

As determined as ever, I held my hand up to Phil to signal "Stop."

"Okay. You want to show me what you can do?" Phil said. "Let's see this."

Holding on to the bed rail, I turned to the side and sat up with my feet over the edge of the bed. I put my left leg, the stronger one, on the floor first. Then my right foot followed.

"Good, stronger foot first."

Next, I slowly stood holding on to the side of the bed.

Phil retrieved my hospital walker resting against the wall.

He placed it in front of me. "Here you go, Bud."

I glanced one more time at the wood block on my table. *"I can do all things through him who strengthens me."* I placed my hands on the walker and stood straight up, slightly away from the bed.

"Now, move the walker just a touch in front of you."

I knew this part. I had done this in physical therapy yesterday.

"There you go! You are walking on your own! Easy with the right leg."

I scooted along toward the bathroom. I repeated the verse over and over in my mind, *"I can do all things through him who strengthens me."* Once inside the bathroom, I stopped close to the door. I needed to hang my pajama top up on the hook. I carefully held on to the walker with one hand and let it slip off. On the other side, I caught the pajama top before it hit the floor and reached for the hook.

"Here, let me get that." Phil reached for my pajama top. "Not sure you can keep your balance and stretch that far. You're doing great. Alex will be pleased with your progress. Now, let's get those pajama bottoms."

I smiled and moved to the shower. Phil steadied the walker and the chair for me as I carefully lowered myself to the shower chair.

"Great job! Now, how about if I get the water going, hand you the soap, and you try the whole shower yourself?"

I nodded and smiled.

Phil started the water, handed me the soap, and stepped outside the door. "Just holler if you need me. Well, you know, don't holler, but you know what I mean."

I knew taking a shower hadn't been a big deal before the wreck. Now, being strong enough to get myself in here and get to the chair was a milestone. My determination paid off. I thought about the Bible verse on the nightstand, and I repeated the verse in my head again and again.

Phil poked his head in the door. "Ready?"

I nodded. He handed me a towel, and a couple of minutes later, he handed me some clothes. I tried to pull on my sweatpants, but I struggled.

Phil steadied me and assisted with the sweatpants. "There you go, Bud. You almost made it."

I reached for the walker and stood for a minute before I began the trek back to my bed. Seeing a nurse wrapping up my old sheets to take to the laundry cart surprised me.

"Good morning, Wes. Your bed is all cleaned up for you."

"Tha–yo," I said.

"You're welcome."

Phil braced the walker as I climbed carefully onto the bed. "Now, would you like to use the shaver yourself today?"

I smiled, nodded, and took the electric shaver. Phil watched for a few seconds and then assisted me in the shaving movements. My grasp wasn't quite strong enough to make a steady movement across my face. But I felt like it wouldn't be long before I could do this alone, too.

Alex appeared as I finished up my shave. "Look at you!"

"That's not all. This guy just walked to the shower and took his own shower."

"Seriously?" Alex asked. "You *are* making progress, Buddy. And now that you're dressed, shall we walk down the hallway? I have the mobility trainer outside the door to help with your balance. Pretty soon, you won't even need that."

Alex walked beside me as I made it to the corner down the hallway. "Want to walk a little more?"

I nodded.

"All right. Let's keep going. Just a few more minutes and we will turn around."

We made it to the next corner, turned around, and walked back to my room.

The assistant met us at the door with my lunch tray. "Thought you'd be ready for this."

I nodded.

The assistant moved my writing papers to my night table.

She sat the lunch tray on my bed tray.

Back on my bed, I pulled the tray closer and uncovered the plate.

"I know," the assistant said. "Doesn't look too good. But it might taste better than it looks."

At least I know Granddad is bringing me dinner. I made a few stabs at some kind of meat and took a couple of bites. I skipped right over to the dessert. Hard to mess up chocolate pudding.

Lorenzo came in. "Hey, Wes. How are you doing? Looks like you have mastered the art of eating with that spoon. It won't be long before you will be using regular utensils." Lorenzo glanced at my papers on the night table. "And you are doing some writing. Hard to hold the pencil?"

I nodded.

"Okay. I'm going to run down to my office and grab some things. I'll be right back."

I finished what I could of my lunch and dessert. I pushed the bed tray aside just as an assistant popped her head through the doorway. "Finished with your lunch?"

I nodded.

Lorenzo returned. "Okay, Wes. Here are some options we can try. See, this one is a simple pencil grip. And here, these are a little more involved. You can put these fingers inside this part, and it will help you hold on to the tip. But the simple grip might be more to your liking, and it will help you until your hand grip is a little stronger. You are almost there."

Lorenzo moved the bed tray back over my lap and put clean pieces of paper in the center. "Let's try each of these and see which one you want to use."

He placed the different grips in my hand, and I attempted to write with each one.

"Looks like you had an easier time with this one, the simple grip."

"Ye–."

He placed the grip in my hand, and I wrote, "Thank you."

"Nice! Oh, and you're welcome. I will bring you a few more

of these. You can keep them to use at home until you feel you are ready to write on your own. Now, let's talk about using a fork. Your wrist control is getting better, and I think you can tackle using a fork and not the rubber spoon. How does that sound?"

I smiled.

"Okay." He held up a fork with a thick, bright blue handle. "This one works like the grip for your pencil. It is fatter than the regular fork handle and you can hold it. But you will have to go slow and be careful when you bring it to your mouth because these ends are pretty sharp. I can leave it for you to try with dinner. What do you think? Want to try it?"

"Ye–"

Lorenzo left, and at last, I thought I would get a much-needed nap. I closed my eyes. Soon, I heard April.

"Good afternoon, Wes. Oh, a fork and pencil grip. Good deal. You are doing well."

"Ye–."

"Okay. We are going to work on your speech now. You are making progress using your words. You intend to use the correct words, which is terrific. I have clients who can say all kinds of words, pronounce them perfectly and everything, but the words make no sense. That means their issue is from the part of the brain that processes speech production or the brain putting the right words in their mouth. You have the right words. Your issue is just speech production and, specifically, following all the way through the word. We need to work on the sounds at the end of words. For the word 'yes,' for example, we need to work on pronouncing the *S* at the end. Okay?"

I nodded.

"Let me hear you make the *S* sound."

I made the sound which surprised me because I hadn't been able to any time I had tried before.

"Okay, now let's put that on the end of the word. Let's try 'yes.'"

I attempted "yes" but the end sound was very faint.

"Okay, let's try again."

I muttered, "Yes, yes."

"Good. Now, I want you to exaggerate the ending *S*. I know it might sound a little funny at first. It will help you develop the habit of saying it all the way through the end of the word. Understand?"

I nodded. I practiced several times until I finally said the *S* loud enough for it to be detected.

"Great! See, you can do this. I want you to do some homework for me and Lorenzo, too. I want you to use your pencil grip, write down a few words, look at the ending, and then read it aloud all the way to the end of the word. Okay?"

I nodded.

"Pick some of the common words you use every day. Like plate, fork, thank you, please, and so on. You pick the words. Then, once you have five or more words, you can practice them several times. Pronounce each word all the way to the end. When I come back tomorrow, we will go over the words again and think up some new ones to practice."

I nodded. So far, a very productive day.

CHAPTER TWENTY-THREE

Checking Out

Granddad returned later along with a patient assistant carrying bags of takeout food.

"Thank you, Miss. You saved the day. That was a workout." He laughed. "She met me at the entrance downstairs."

"You're welcome," she said. "I couldn't let you struggle like you were. Glad I could help. Have a good evening."

I took the pencil with the pencil grip and wrote, "What is it?"

"Nice writing! You have a new pencil. That's a pretty cool gadget. Hmm, you mean what's in the bags?"

"Yes."

"Oh, my goodness, you said the whole word 'yes!'" He smiled. "I have a variety of things in here from the Country Cookin' Kitchen. You have your pick. Your parents made suggestions and said they would take whatever plates you didn't want. Each plate has potatoes, vegetables, a salad, and bread. You pick from…" He held up each bag and then identified their contents, "Chicken-fried steak, fried chicken, hamburger steak with gravy, or catfish and fries."

What a hard choice. I liked them all. I had attempted the hospital's version of fried chicken and chicken-fried steak. It kind of ruined my appetite for eating them again. I opted to try the catfish.

My parents entered the room.

"Thanks, Dad, for picking up everyone's dinner," Dad said.

"Happy to do it."

Everyone sorted out who wanted each dinner plate, and the room fell quiet.

"Wes," Dad said, "You're using a fork!"

"Yes," I said.

"What next? Talking better, using a fork. What will you do tomorrow?"

Dr. Arnold opened the door and answered my father's question. "I will tell you what he will do tomorrow. He is going home."

Now I couldn't even chew. This news overwhelmed me. *Home at last.*

"That is wonderful news, Dr. Arnold," my father responded.

"Yes, Wes, your therapies are paying off. You are still a little unstable when you walk. But your physical therapist will visit you at home a couple of times a week to work on that. You will get your cast off and use a brace and crutches. Alex feels strongly you will manage with a brace, crutches, and later, a cane as you gain your strength and balance back. And you were able to shower, assisted with dressing, I think outpatient therapy is all you need for now. I will ask you to come back in two weeks and let me check you over. You can call my office and they will arrange the appointment."

My face wouldn't stop smiling the entire time we finished our dinner.

Mom put all the dinner containers into a bag and took them down the hall to the large trash can by the nurse's station. My father and Granddad discussed getting me back and forth to the outpatient therapy center for the immediate future.

"Let me take care of him during the week while you are both at work. It would be great to have his company," Granddad said.

Dad turned to me. "Will that work for you, Wes?"

Home? Are you serious?

I couldn't stop smiling. "Yes."

"Great. Tomorrow, Mom and I will come by and check you in the morning. I suppose we will get the therapy schedule for the outpatient treatment then."

Not long after the discussion, Granddad, Mom, and Dad left. Tomorrow would be a big day.

I changed out of my sweats and into my pajamas without too many problems. My dressing skills were improving, but I had not yet had to try buttons or zippers. Sweats, pajamas, and a hospital gown were not too difficult.

Settling down under the covers, I heard a tiny knock on my door.

"Wes?"

I recognized the voice. *Carol Ann.*

She slowly peeked inside the door. "Okay if I come in?"

"Yes."

"You sound stronger," she said.

I smiled and nodded.

"I just wanted to stop by and see how you are doing."

My brain sent the word "better" to my mouth. "Be–t–."

"Better? Great!"

I smiled.

"I forgot to tell you my phone number the other day. I wanted you to have it in case you need anything, anything at all."

I smiled. She was very sweet. I motioned to the paper and pencil on the night table. She wrote her number on the paper. I motioned for her to hand me another piece of paper and the pencil. She handed me the pencil with the grip and a clean sheet of paper. "Going home tomorrow," I wrote.

"That is amazing! And so is your writing. Look at that cool pencil with the blue thing on it. I'll bet that helps."

"Yes," I said.

"Good. And you are talking better?"

"Yes."

"Is there anything you need now?"

I shook my head no. Then I remembered I needed to give her my phone number. I held up my hand and said, "Wai–t."

I wrote down my phone number as fast as I could.

Carol Ann approached me, took the paper with my number, and gave me a quick hug. "Great, thanks. Just call me or text if you need something."

I nodded.

It didn't take long to fall asleep after Carol Ann left. I slept most of the night except for when a nurse came in to check on me. She left quietly, and I dozed again.

The cheery morning nurse came in, as usual, to open the window curtain and take my vitals. "Good morning, Wes. Heard you are leaving us today?"

"Yes."

"We will miss you, but I know you're glad to be going home. Now, do you want to shower before we take your cast off or just dress for home?"

"Show..ur." I forced the sound at the end of the word.

"Perfect. I'll get Juan."

After my shower, Juan helped me partially get dressed. We waited for the cast removal before I added my sweatpants.

"Good. There you go," Juan said. "I'll let Alex know you are ready to get that thing off your leg."

I huge smile emerged. I had no control. It would be wonderful to get it off.

Moments later, Alex came in with the medical assistant to remove the cast.

Before Alex left, another nurse popped in and said, "Good morning, Wes. Oh, getting that cast off. Good deal. Here are your discharge papers. Someone will bring in a breakfast tray in a couple of minutes. Your parents coming to pick you up?"

"Yes."

"Okay."

Alex, the assistant, and the nurse left as Granddad entered the door. The nurse greeted him. "Good morning, Mr. Williams."

"Good morning," Granddad said. "No cast? That's terrific!"

"Hi, Gran–" I sputtered.

"That's my boy." He smiled. "Did I ever tell you about the time I couldn't hear anyone talking when I was in Korea?"

I shook my head.

"It was very interesting trying to talk when I couldn't hear. It took several days for my ears to return to, well, as normal as they are now." He laughed. "Anyway, I wanted so badly for people to know what I wanted or what I was thinking, I would just blurt something out. Sometimes it made no sense whatsoever. I know it's frustrating for you, too. You want to say something, and you can't get it out. But you can say the right words when you speak. Now, how about a donut and a cup of coffee before that tray arrives with some unidentifiable breakfast slop?"

I smiled and eagerly ate a glazed donut.

My parents followed Alex into my room. He had a small brace and a set of crutches with him.

"Good morning, everyone," Alex said. "Let's try this brace out before you leave."

Once the brace was on, Alex handed me a set of crutches and helped me stand using the crutches. I felt a little weak, but more independent.

"That's it. There you go buddy." Alex said.

I practiced a few more steps, smiling all the while.

The nurse returned to the room and parked a wheelchair close to my bed.

"Mom and Dad, you will be bringing the car to the door?"

"Yes," Dad said.

"Great, let me know when you are ready, and I will take Wes downstairs. Just buzz me at the nurse's station."

I tucked the small Bible Carol Ann had given me into my pocket along with the paper with Carol Ann's number on it. I grabbed the pencil with the grip and the adaptive fork. Mom packed my other belongings in a plastic bag the nurse brought into the room.

The discharge process required a couple of things before my parents had approval for my release. For one thing, they had to rent some equipment. The rentals included a wheelchair to use on uneven spaces or going away to places like the store and a very un-attractive shower chair.

Thankfully, things moved quickly. My parents looked over the discharge papers while we waited on my breakfast tray.

"Look, Dad." My dad nudged my grandfather and pointed at something on the paper. "The address of the outpatient therapy center. It's in the shopping center near the Donut Shop."

"Well, Wes, I guess you know what that means." Granddad winked.

I smiled. I knew that meant, at least two days a week, we would go to the Donut Shop.

"And, it says here, Wes," Dad continued, "the therapist at the center will refer you back to the doctor for clearance to return to school. You'll be able to finish the last few weeks of your senior year after all."

This was good news that I hadn't really considered. I hadn't been able to do schoolwork yet, but, in my final semester, I only had two classes left, anyway. I had completed all my major school credits last semester. I had only Art and an extra Graphic Design class I had signed up for as fun. But it would be nice to see my friends again.

Mom looked over the discharge papers next. "Wes, do you know you have been here for over two months?"

I was stunned. I knew it had been a long time. I didn't realize it had been that long.

"Two months, one week, and four days, to be exact," Mom added.

I was curious how much of that time I was in a near-death experience? How long was I in a coma? Maybe I could find out someday.

The ride in the wheelchair to the front door didn't take long. Once through the front door, I couldn't help but feel like I was about to cry. I wasn't sad about leaving the hospital. My imminent tears were tears of joy. I felt the breeze, saw the sun, and heard birds again. I knew from the date on my discharge papers that it was early spring. I had forgotten how wonderful it felt to be outdoors in the fresh spring air.

The nurse wheeled me out to my parents' car. Granddad stood nearby.

"I will see you the day after tomorrow," Granddad said.

"Yes."

I gazed out the car window. The views astonished me. I

had taken everything for granted in the past. The road toward my house always had a couple of pastures. I hadn't paid attention to the wildflowers, the number of cattle, and the longhorn steers along the fence. The best view was the one I caught as Dad turned the car onto my street. Each house on the block had its own characteristic charm. I knew the families who lived here. I knew how they cared for their yards and their own families. It felt cozy somehow.

Dad turned and drove up our driveway. Our house, which sat on a small hill, was surrounded by trees and beautiful flower beds. Great relief washed over me. I was home at last.

CHAPTER TWENTY-FOUR

Legal Issues

The first day at my house went by quickly. Mom had taken off work to get me settled, and Dad stayed home and helped with my shower. He had already moved my bed to a different location in my room to make a clear path to the bathroom. He arranged everything I needed and thought about each piece of furniture and placed it strategically so I could easily get around to the other side of my bed.

With a little help from Dad to steady the shower chair, I would be able to get into the shower and wash and then dress myself. I hoped the next few weeks wouldn't be like when I was four or five years old all over again. I halfway expected Dad would want to check behind my ears to see if I missed a spot.

Mom had placed the clothes I needed after my shower on the new hook Dad had installed by my bathroom door. So far, I had adjusted to being home very easily. And I certainly had no trouble adjusting to home-cooked food again. Mom had always been a great cook.

"Wes, you ready for dinner?" Mom called.

"We will be right there," Dad replied. He assisted me out of the shower chair, and I took over my dressing routine.

Once Dad said a blessing for the food, Mom passed the bowls of food around and I scooped out my helpings. Dad placed a chicken breast from the platter onto my plate.

"Wes," Mom said, "Do you think you would be up for meeting with the attorney in the morning? Dad and I already took tomorrow off work, and we can take you down to his office."

The entire idea about hiring an attorney to file charges against Carol Ann was not something I wanted. I thought the best thing to do was meet with Mr. Keller directly and let him know how I felt. I wanted to get this part over with. I wanted to put the accident in the past and move on. Having a near-death experience made me appreciate everything. I had been given a second chance at life, and I didn't intend to use my time dragging out a criminal charge or a lawsuit against anyone. I knew now that life could end in a second. I knew my life had changed in an instant. And I knew God had given me this chance and I wanted to make a positive difference, not ruin people's lives.

I nodded at Mom.

"You feel up to going tomorrow?"

"Yes."

I figured it would be too difficult to explain things to my parents. And I didn't want to attempt to get my thoughts across to them tonight and then the attorney tomorrow. I would try to communicate tomorrow when we were all together at the attorney's office.

"Okay, Wes. The appointment is set for ten in the morning. We should be able to get there by then."

I nodded.

My parents talked during dinner about the yard and other things they planned to do this spring. Spring was the time Mom enjoyed doing improvements around the house. It would be fun to see what she had in mind. And until I was cleared to go to school, I could witness her efforts.

Nighttime was unusual. I woke several times before the sun was up. I expected nurses to be entering my room at any moment. But they didn't. Then I remembered I was home and drifted back to sleep. Mom didn't wake me until almost eight o'clock.

"Good morning, honey. I'm making pancakes for you."

That sounds delicious. I took my crutches by the side of my bed and put my feet on the floor. It didn't take me too long to get up and grab my robe.

I was right. Mom's homemade pancakes were as delicious as

I had imagined. After a second cup of coffee, Dad assisted me in getting dressed. It seemed each day was easier, and I did more by myself.

Today, I not only mostly dressed myself, but I remembered the small Bible and put it in my pocket. I wanted to write down my own thoughts for the attorney, so I grabbed the pencil with the grip on it from the hospital.

"It looks like everyone is ready on time," Dad said as I made my way down the hallway with my crutches. "Wes, you want to get started to the driveway?"

I nodded.

I knew where Mr. Keller's office was downtown, but it was as if I were sightseeing. Our town, like many small towns, had a town square with quaint old buildings with unique shops and cafés all around. I enjoyed seeing the town square once again. Mr. Keller's office was on Main Street, just one block off the square.

"I'll pull up to the curb so you and your mother can get out by the door before I park the car."

"That sounds good," Mom said.

Mom and I made our way inside and sat in the small lobby. Dad joined us quickly. "Found a spot right out front," he said.

"Good morning," Mr. Keller's receptionist said. She escorted us to his office. It was a large room with bookshelves that reached to the ceiling. I don't believe I'd ever seen so many books except in the high school library. We sat around a large wooden table in the center of the room.

"It is good to see you out and about, Wes."

I nodded.

"Now, I have a document here showing the possible charges that might be filed in the case. I believe the evidence is clear. I also think Carol Ann and her parents may wish to settle this out of court to avoid any possible legal charges about her texting while driving. How do you feel about this? We can insist on the charges if you like."

I shook my head no and gestured for the yellow legal tablet next to him.

I wrote, "No charges. I want nothing from Carol Ann."

I handed Mr. Keller the tablet.

"Wes, are you sure? Mr. and Mrs. Williams, are you in agreement?"

Dad looked at me and said, "Son, now, let's think about this. It will cost money for all your treatments, and you might have side effects from this accident the rest of your life."

This made me smile. I knew the accident would affect the rest of my life, but not like Dad meant. I knew the accident gave me a second chance and the rest of my life would definitely be changed, but for the better.

Dad's expression told me he didn't understand what I was thinking about. "Son, is there something we don't know?"

Since I was still writing large letters, I flipped the tablet to a clean page and wrote "Insurance for treatment?" and passed the tablet back to Mr. Keller.

Mr. Keller looked at the paper. "Wes, I know your parents have medical insurance for your hospital treatments. But are you asking about insurance money for treatment from Carol Ann?"

"Yes."

"Yes, her parents have agreed to use their insurance money so your family will not have any outstanding medical expenses. Is that what you meant?"

I replied, "Yes."

Puzzled, Mr. Keller said, "I don't understand. Most people would be eager to get as much money as possible for an accident like this."

I shook my head.

"Are you sure? You could buy a more expensive car than you could with your own car insurance money."

Mom and Dad looked disappointed. I knew they wanted the best for me. But it didn't feel right. I wasn't given a second chance at life to get money from Carol Ann and her family.

Mr. Keller said, "I don't understand. What is it you want?"

I wrote, "Nothing. She is sorry."

Mr. Keller truly didn't like this answer and asked once more.

"Surely there is something you might want money for. College?"

"No," I replied.

"Why?" Mr. Keller asked.

I flipped the tablet page again and wrote, "I have texted, too."

"Think about it, Son," Dad said. Both he and Mom looked bewildered.

Underneath what I just wrote, I added, "Log in my eye."

Mom started to cry.

"I don't understand," Mr. Keller said.

Dad nodded and smiled. "Okay, son. Mr. Keller, it's from a Bible story. It is when Jesus said we aren't to find fault in others, like a spec in someone's eye, when we have a log in our own eye. He means he can't condemn Carol Ann for something he has done before." Dad turned to me and said, "I could not be prouder of you than I am at this very moment."

CHAPTER TWENTY-FIVE

My Second Chance

Mr. Keller's office told us they would contact Carol Ann's parents that afternoon to let them know the charges would not be filed and nothing further would happen. No one knew yet if the state would file charges against Carol since it was against the law in Texas to text while driving.

Carol Ann sent me a text first thing the next day.

Heard about the meeting yesterday with Mr. Keller. Thank you so much for not going further with the accident.

I could see she was typing another message and her next text came through before I could finish my attempt to reply.

Now, I have only the hearing on the ticket written about the accident next week. I will likely be fined, and I am not sure what else yet. But it helps to know your family will not ask for more money.

It took me a while, and several tries to respond to her text. At last, I clumsily typed out,

I know one thing for sure. I won't text and drive ever again. I smiled.

Me either. Thank you again.

I hesitated for a moment and then texted her again.

You think we might get together again soon? Maybe coffee and talk? I waited for her next reply.

That would be great. Just let me know when.

I couldn't help but smile, thinking about her. I hoped to see her before long.

My parents and grandfather worked out the outpatient therapy schedule. My therapy would be twice a week until I regained my strength, balance, and speech. I vowed not to miss a single session. The therapy center wasn't far from my house and, coincidentally, was next door to the Donut Shop. My grandfather and I planned to stop in for donuts following the therapy sessions and I promised to never miss a Saturday when Old Walt, Parker, and Lawson could join us.

The first Saturday Granddad took me to the Donut Shop, the clapping and whistling of the men and the others in the shop was deafening. Using my crutches to get into the shop gave everyone looking out of the window plenty of time to prepare for their loudest clapping and whistling.

"There he is!" Old Walt said.

Before I could get to the table, Jae brought my donuts and coffee and said, "You look good."

Parker stood up and pulled out my chair. "About time you came back."

Walter laughed and said, "I thought you didn't like us anymore."

And Lawson simply hugged me and said, "Hey, Wes."

The stories and jokes continued as if I had never missed a single Saturday. In truth, it had been over three months since I had been in the Donut Shop. But this time, it felt different. Jimmy was noticeably absent, and I realized now how much I missed him. I sat at the familiar table and took in every smell, every sound, every story, and every joke. I valued this time much more than I had in the past.

My eighteenth birthday came and went with little fanfare. My mother was very sentimental, saying how blessed we were that I had lived to see eighteen. Me? I didn't feel much different from the last day I was seventeen. But, unlike other years, this year I felt blessed to live each single day and planned to be a better person than the day before.

Unlike any other time in my life, I was concerned about my future. I practiced my speech drills daily every single day. I needed to have my speech restored completely before the next school year. I wasn't certain where I would go to college, but I was determined to attend.

For the rest of the school year, I was blessed to have assistance and support through the special services department of the high school. It began a few weeks after I came home from the hospital. My teachers came by my house twice a week with makeup assignments. Between therapy schedules, home tutoring, and meeting with Granddad and his buddies, the time passed fairly quickly.

I caught up on my schoolwork, and the doctor cleared me to return to school for the last month of my senior year. It was great to see my friends again. But my school friends seemed to be, well, so young. I guess there is a part of a person that matures quickly once you must fight for your life. Going over to an out-of-body state and returning aged me somehow. But I think it aged me in a good way.

As the end of the school year approached, I wondered if Carol Ann might be ready to get together. I felt enough time had passed. I picked up my phone and texted.

Hi Carol Ann.

Hi, Wes. How are you?

By this time, texting was easier for me. I promptly replied,

Good. Walking with only a cane I use occasionally. How are you?

Good. I paid a fine for texting. All that is behind me.

That's great. Want to meet for coffee tomorrow?

Yes, I would like that.

Donut Shop or Coffee Shop downtown?

Perfect. Coffee shop after school. About 4:30?

Feeling relief and excitement, I texted back,

Sounds good. Oh, Carol Ann?

Yes?

Don't text while driving.

A laughing emoji followed. Then,

Promise I won't.

Since my right leg was still a little weak, I was not driving yet. The insurance company had paid for my new car, but it sat in the driveway for now. My friend Steve, who lived down the street and over one block, was my primary source of transportation. I asked him to drop me off at the coffee shop after school. Mom said she would come by and pick me up after she left work.

I hadn't been to the coffee shop in a while, and it was nice to return. Carol Ann was waiting at a table when I arrived.

"You beat me here," I said and pulled out a chair.

"Yes, I had an early dismissal at school. Some kind of teacher training. Can I order something for you?"

"Oh, I forgot to order when I came in." I sputtered nervously as I sat down. "I just came right over to the table. Sorry. I should have ordered."

"No problem. What would you like?"

"Just a black coffee would be great."

Carol Ann went to the counter, ordered the coffee, and returned. "Here you are."

"Thank you."

"Your speech has improved a lot since I last saw you. I'm glad. It's great to see you up and walking, too."

"Thanks. Lots of hard work to get here, but it's good. It's great to see you. How is school going?"

"Great. Back on the honor roll. I had a tough time at first."

"Thankfully, I'm only taking two classes. That is all I have left before graduation."

"Oh, yes. I guess you are going away to school next year?"

"Haven't planned where, yet."

Our conversation shifted from small talk to what we'd been through. I told her about the first time I saw her standing in the doorway of my hospital room and how I thought she was an angel or a dream. She blushed. We talked for quite a long time until I saw Mom pull into the coffee shop parking lot.

"Oh, there is my ride," I said and gathered my coffee cup and napkin.

"Wait," Carol Ann said, placing her hand on mine.

"Yes?"

"Can we see each other again?"

"Of course. You say when," I smiled.

"How about Monday?"

"I will see you then. Same time?"

"Yes. And thank you for inviting me to meet up."

I stood up and hugged her.

Carol Ann and I met again on Monday. After that, we agreed to meet after school every day that I didn't have therapy. There was something amazing about Carol Ann and our conversations. We talked about everything under the sun. Our after-school meetings at the coffee shop went on for hours.

Two times a week after school, I went to therapy. Using only a cane instead of crutches, I set a goal for my treatment. I wanted to walk across the stage at graduation without a cane. I practiced daily at home. I knew I was close. I knew I could do it. I prayed about my healing each day.

At long last, the day of my high school graduation arrived. Carol Ann sat in the audience with my parents, Granddad, and, of course, Parker, Walt, and Lawson. When my name was called, I think I heard the whistles and screams of the guys from the Donut Shop over the entire crowd. I proudly walked across the stage without my cane and only needed to hold on to the rail to get up and down the stairs. I walked at a regular pace and held my head high. When the principal handed me my diploma, tears filled my eyes as I pointed upward to heaven. It was only through God and His power and grace that I'd lived through the semester and walked across that stage without any assistance.

After the ceremony, Jae opened up the Donut Shop just for our private party. She asked her cousin to help her cater the affair and, for dessert, of course, we had heaping piles of donuts and lots of coffee drinks. I am not sure who enjoyed it more—Granddad, my parents, Granddad's buddies, or me.

Granddad pulled me aside and said, "You know how proud I am of you right now? You came through everything, all the struggles of this year, and achieved your goal. You are a fighter. You fought back when the odds were against you. God gave you that strength. Proud of you, son."

I nodded and said, "Thanks, Granddad. I just wish Grandma and Jimmy were here with us to celebrate."

"I know they are smiling down on us right now, son."

By summer, Carol Ann and I had decided we would start to

date. I was able to drive to her house and pick her up, and other times, she came to pick me up. We visited each other's churches, we met each other's families, and we met each other's friends. We both wanted our relationship to be about more than surviving a wreck. We visited with our parents and both of our pastors before we decided we thought it would be a good idea to make our relationship official.

Whenever someone asked Carol Ann how we met, she'd smile and say, "I just kind of ran into him one day."

If someone asked me how I met Carol Ann, I replied, "Our paths just collided."

Every time Carol Ann and I were together, I felt stronger feelings for her. I even wondered if I was crazy enough about her to climb down in a well and almost get blown up just to have money for a ring. Lawson's story always made me smile.

CHAPTER TWENTY-SIX

The Whole Story

The Saturday following my graduation, Granddad and I had coffee with the guys at the Donut Shop. When we left, I asked Granddad if we could visit out on his porch. I told him I had something to talk to him about.

"Of course, let's go. We haven't had a one-on-one visit in a while on the porch."

I settled in the rocking chair on his front porch. He brought out two cups of coffee.

"Here you go," he said. "What's up? Worried about college or Carol Ann?"

"No, Granddad, I'm not worried about anything at all. I wanted to tell you the whole story of what happened to me in the hospital. I haven't told you everything that happened after the wreck."

"Oh? I didn't realize you remembered that time."

"I haven't told anyone this story. I think I will tell my parents after I tell you. And probably someday I will tell Carol Ann the whole story."

"Okay."

"Not sure how to start, so I just will say it right out. It is hard to explain. But I want to try. When I was in the hospital immediately after the wreck, I think I died."

"Oh, yes, they needed to get your heart beating again."

"But it was before that."

"Really?"

"Yes. I have no idea how it happened, when I was in the hos-

LEGENDS OF THE DONUT SHOP

pital room after the first surgery, from up above my bed, I looked down on myself. It was like I was floating up near the ceiling."

"I've heard of other people who had similar experiences. How did you feel?"

"Scared. I couldn't tell if I was going to live or die. I watched the second surgery, too. But it was strange because I was afraid, but at the same time, it was peaceful somehow. That peaceful feeling was one of accepting whatever was happening. The scene below, seeing myself lying there, looking so lifeless, was frightening. Then they took me back to the operating room."

"No wonder you were afraid. The operating room has to be a scary place."

"In my hospital room, the doctor told my parents I would need another operation. I saw Mom and Dad and tried to tell them it would be okay. But I couldn't move. And then, this is the strangest part, the part I don't understand. Something took me to another place and time. I saw myself, but I was younger, and I saw you, and Parker, Old Walt, Lawson, and I saw Jimmy. He was living then. I think I was about twelve years old."

"That was quite a vision."

"Yes, it was the only thing I held on to because it made me feel good. I heard many of the same stories I'd heard before when I was that age and even a little older. It was incredible to see us all again laughing and joking, and Jimmy living."

"Good old Jimmy. I miss that fellow." Granddad looked down and remained silent. Then he added, "I suppose I hadn't had my hip surgery then?"

"No, you hadn't."

The sadness on Granddad's face could not be overlooked. I knew it was hard for him to think about his disability now. I gave him a moment.

"And there was something else. I heard a voice, not *a* voice, THE Voice. I knew it was God. He told me I was going to live and come back to Him much later."

Granddad smiled. "If anyone knows when it is your time to stay on earth or go to Heaven, it's Him. I'll bet you will live a long time and you will have a good life. I certainly have. And plan to keep on for years." He laughed.

"Granddad, do you remember the day at the Donut Shop when we were talking about having a purpose in life? And then we came back here, and we talked about how you had made it home from Korea and so many of your friends died in that war and what you knew was your purpose after the war?"

"Yes, I think you were about fifteen or sixteen then?"

"Yes. I was fifteen."

"And now, you're eighteen and starting college. Have you thought more about your plans? Your purpose?"

"Back then, you told me your survival of the war changed your life. You decided the most important thing was to live a good life and have a strong faith."

"You remembered all that?"

"Yes, and I saw it all again when I was in the near-death state. That is what I wanted to tell you. My experience of almost dying, of somehow being in a state of afterlife or near-death for so long, changed me. My faith is stronger. I realize what's important. And you were right. I know all I need is to have strong faith and everything else will take care of itself. I will study, find a job, and, who knows, maybe Carol Ann and I will become more serious about our relationship. But I know God will help me with all of that because I have faith that He will."

"Yes, son, He will. If you believe, and get close to Him, He will get close to you."

"Yes sir."

"Any inkling of an idea what you want to do as a career someday?"

"Not certain, but I'm thinking about going into ministry or counseling or even some type of therapy to help people who have been in car accidents or had strokes."

"Any of those sound just fine. You would be terrific in any of those careers, helping others."

We sat and finished our coffee and watched the flags blowing in the breeze flying high on the pole by the driveway. I treasured these moments. I felt optimistic about my future, and I knew I would have the strength to do whatever God planned for me.

Epilogue

Carol Ann took advanced courses in high school and caught up with me in college. Five years after the accident, we both graduated from college. Carol Ann and I were engaged during our second year of college and decided we would marry before graduate school. We had both been accepted to graduate programs. I would enroll in the Divinity and Missionary graduate program and Carol Ann would study Christian Counseling.

I proposed to Carol Ann over a memorable dinner at one of our favorite hangouts, and she said "yes" without hesitation. The best part was I didn't have to dig a well to come up with the money for the ring.

We were married in a beautiful church ceremony in my hometown. Granddad, although in declining health, was my best man. My dad wheeled him right up to the front of the church. The remaining members of the group, Old Walt, Parker, and Lawson, had hosted a bachelor party for me at the Donut Shop the week before I got married. Jae prepared a special menu of Korean food for the party. I was blessed that all these men could gather once again in one of my favorite places. Not long afterward, Lawson went to Heaven, followed by Old Walt. Parker lived in a nursing home, and I visited whenever I could until he passed away.

When Carol Ann and I completed our graduate studies, we accepted a call as a pastor and a pastoral counselor at a midsize church outside of Fort Worth. During our first year at the church, Carol Ann and I had our first son. We would later have another son and a daughter.

Ten years after the wreck that changed the paths of our lives forever, Granddad passed away. I knew he was in Heaven with my grandmother. I also suspected that on each Saturday, he and the rest of the Donut Shop gang went to a donut shop in Heaven together and told stories and jokes. I miss him.

Made in the USA
Coppell, TX
20 March 2022

75290427R00083